FAVORITES FROM CHRIS GRABENSTEIN

The Island of Dr. Libris
No Is All I Know
No More Naps!
Shine! (coauthored with J.J. Grabenstein)

MR. LEMONCELLO'S LIBRARY SERIES

Mr. Lemoncello's Very First Game
Escape from Mr. Lemoncello's Library
Mr. Lemoncello's Library Olympics
Mr. Lemoncello's Great Library Race
Mr. Lemoncello's All-Star Breakout Game
Mr. Lemoncello and the Titanium Ticket

THE SMARTEST KID IN THE UNIVERSE SERIES

The Smartest Kid in the Universe
Genius Camp
Evil Genius

DOG SQUAD SERIES

Dog Squad
Dog Squad 2: Cat Crew

SMARTEST KID IN THE UNIVERSE

EVIL GENIUS

CHRIS GRABENSTEIN

RANDOM HOUSE 🏠 NEW YORK

Text copyright © 2023 by Chris Grabenstein
Jacket art copyright © 2023 by Antoine Losty
Title lettering copyright © 2023 by Neil Swaab

Visit us on the Web! rhcbooks.com

Educators and librarians, for a variety of teaching tools, visit us at RHTeachersLibrarians.com

Library of Congress Cataloging-in-Publication Data
Name: Grabenstein, Chris, author.
Title: Evil genius / Chris Grabenstein.
Description: First edition. | New York: Random House Children's Books, [2023] | Series: The smartest kid in the universe; book 3 | Audience: Ages 8–12. | Summary: Twelve-year-old Jake McQuade is the smartest kid in the universe, but if he wants to keep his title he will have to figure out a way to defeat the villain who steals his ingestible knowledge capsules.
Identifiers: LCCN 2022009210 (print) | LCCN 2022009211 (ebook) | ISBN 978-0-593-48091-5 (trade) | ISBN 978-0-593-48092-2 (lib. bdg.) | ISBN 978-0-593-70505-6 (int'l) | ISBN 978-0-593-48094-6 (ebook)
Subjects: CYAC: Genius—Fiction. | Stealing—Fiction. | Middle schools—Fiction. | Schools—Fiction. | Humorous stories. | LCGFT: Humorous fiction. | Novels.
Classification: LCC PZ7.G7487 Ev 2023 (print) | LCC PZ7.G7487 (ebook) | DDC [Fic]—dc23

The text of this book is set in 11.5-point Sabon LT Pro.
Interior design by Megan Shortt

Printed in the United States of America
1st Printing
First Edition

In memory of my mom,
Christine Lemonopoulos Grabenstein
1926–2022
"Being gifted doesn't mean you've been given something.
It means you have something to give."

PROLOGUE

As captain, Aliento de Perro knew he was supposed to go down with his sinking ship.

But he was a pirate.

Pirates weren't big on obeying the rules.

A British man-o'-war had just fired a cannon blast that snapped his boat's mizzenmast in two. Splinters and red-hot cinders rained down onto the deck. The sky was on fire.

Fortunately, the chicken-hearted cabin boy Eduardo Leones was already rowing upriver in a small dinghy, ferrying a heavy treasure chest filled with plunder. Gold. Jewelry. Precious artifacts. Everything the ship known as the *Stinky Dog* had pillaged during its seven-year voyage.

Well, almost everything.

Eduardo's father had been the original capitán of the

pirate ship. He was the one responsible for collecting most of its riches. That changed when De Perro led a mutiny that ended with Capitán Leones walking the plank.

Now it was De Perro's turn to jump overboard.

He would probably never see the cabin boy or the treasure chest again.

But that didn't matter.

Because young Eduardo didn't have *all* the *Stinky Dog*'s loot. The most precious item was still on board.

¡La Gran Calabaza!

The Big Pumpkin.

An orange diamond as round and large as the British cannonballs whizzing through the air. It was worth more than all the other pirate booty combined.

The gigantic gemstone sat nestled in a bed of dry straw, locked inside a plain metal box.

Capitán De Perro tucked that treasure chest under an arm and made his way to the railing. The ship's bow tilted skyward. Its stern sank deeper into the harbor.

Aliento de Perro, whose name meant "Dog Breath," turned to face his scrambling crew.

"¡Hasta luego, tontos!" he shouted.

"Arrrr!" Several of the pirates cringed and covered their noses. When Dog Breath shouted, anyone within a fathom could smell how he'd earned his name.

The capitán leapt into the turbulent waters below. He landed with a mighty splash, went under for an instant, and bobbed back to the surface. He grabbed hold of a drifting piece of wood and kicked hard, making his way through a sea of fiery debris. He was headed toward a rocky, oyster-rich island he knew of at the mouth of the bay.

Aliento de Perro had a plan.

He'd bury his treasure deep within that island's craggy crust. He'd hide it well and mark the spot.

And one day, after he'd escaped from whatever prison cage his English captors tossed him into, he'd come back and retrieve la Gran Calabaza.

Hours after hiding his precious treasure on the small island, Aliento de Perro was seized by British sailors. They locked him in irons and transported him across the ocean to London, where he was jailed inside Newgate Prison.

The pirate wasn't there very long before he was tried, convicted, and sentenced to death by hanging.

Capitán De Perro's last visitor, before the prison chaplain arrived to escort him to the gallows, was his son Huberto.

Who told *his* son what his father had told him.

When that son became a father, he too passed along the family's secret.

And so it went for generation after generation.

But to this day, no descendant of Aliento de Perro had ever done his bidding.

None had ever unraveled his riddle.

None had ever found the giant orange diamond known as la Gran Calabaza.

1

The clock was ticking.

Jake McQuade was on a mission for the top-secret agency known as the Consortium. The twelve-year-old had already defeated the world's most sophisticated artificially intelligent computer and solved impossible cases for the FBI—and, thanks to his newfound knowledge of geometry, physics, and human psychology, he'd also starred on his middle school basketball team.

His pale, freckled skin baked in the scorching midday sun. He was on a high-speed rigid-hull inflatable boat zooming across choppy waters with a small team of commandos in scuba gear. His mother had been right: Jake should've packed sunscreen.

The commando team dropped Jake and his best friend, Kojo Shelton, on a craggy island.

"You two are on your own," said the squad commander, clicking a stopwatch. "You have fifteen minutes to secure the package."

Jake used a handheld mapping device to quickly find the target building.

But inside the windowless structure, things slowed down. The place was like a dark maze trapped inside a fun house.

Except this house was more dangerous than fun.

Jake and Kojo followed the blinking green dot through a series of switchbacks and found themselves trapped inside a black box of a room. The instant their feet hit the floor, a huge metal door slammed shut behind them.

"We need to get out of this room, Jake," said Kojo, checking his glowing watch. "Fast! We only have ten more minutes to secure the package."

"Working on it," said Jake. He was thinking. Trying to come up with a solution.

"Where to next?"

"I'm, uh, not sure."

"What? Come on. Use your big jelly-beaned brain."

This mission was, clearly, a test of Jake's superior intellect.

And that made him a little nervous.

Jake hadn't become super intelligent the usual way—studying, reading books, doing homework. He'd taken a shortcut: Ingestible Knowledge capsules in the form of jelly beans.

Jake never knew if or when his mental superpowers would disappear.

He just hoped it wasn't today.

2

"**O**h, wow, check it out," said Kojo, rustling around inside the sleek nylon sling bag the Consortium had given them for this mission. "There's all sorts of cool gear in here. Duct tape. A Swiss Army knife. A pair of binoculars. Hold up. I think there're some Hershey bars in here, too." He sniffed loudly. "Oh yeah. That's chocolate." Another sniff. "This one has almonds."

"Great," mumbled Jake. He was distracted. His whole mind was focused on the mapping device. But the green dot in the center of the grid had stopped moving. All it was doing now was blinking.

"Looks like that thing's busted," said Kojo, peering over Jake's shoulder.

Jake nodded, even though he wasn't sure Kojo was right.

He needed time.

To study the sequence of blinks.

"Two long, one short," he muttered. "Three long. Long, short, short, short, short . . ."

"You thinking about pants?" said Kojo. "Shirtsleeves?"

"Nope."

Jake reached into his own nylon sling bag. He shoved aside the binoculars and pulled out a spiral notebook and a pen.

"It's Morse code. Short blinks and long blinks. Dots and dashes."

"Cool," said Kojo, biting off a chunk of chocolate bar.

Jake wrote down the sequence of light flashes. He knew Morse code from a book he'd skimmed a couple of weeks ago.

--. --- / - .... .-. --- ..- --. .... / - .... . /
-.. --- --- .-. / .. -. / - .... . / ..-. .-.. --- --- .-.

"What's it mean?" asked Kojo.

"Go through the door in the floor."

"There's a door in the floor?" said Kojo. "Who designed this building?"

Jake and Kojo dropped to their knees. The room was so dark, they'd have to feel their way to any kind of hidden doorway. They patted around with their hands.

"Got it!" said Kojo, pulling up and twisting a ring latch.

He yanked on it.

It opened. Jake peered in. Once his eyes adjusted, he saw another room directly below the room they were in.

That was where they needed to be.

But first they'd have to get past the web of criss-crossing laser beams.

3

"Those lasers are a trip wire!" said Kojo, looking down at the web of thin green beams. "Just like in *Mission: Impossible*. The movie, not the TV show. Although Eartha Kitt *did* evade a bank vault's light sensors in season one of the TV show."

Jake looked at Kojo. His best friend streamed a lot of old-school TV. He'd even adopted the "Who loves you, baby?" catchphrase of the 1970s Tootsie Pops–loving TV detective Kojak.

"We might be soul mates," Kojo had once told Jake. "He's Ko-*jak* and I'm Ko-*jo*. Sure, he's a bald, old Greek dude and I'm a handsome, young Black dude, but come on—we both dig Tootsie Pops."

"We can't just drop down into the room," said Jake.

"Well, duh," said Kojo. "You break those laser beams,

they're gonna set off some kind of alarm. Even I know that, and I haven't eaten a single one of Mr. Farooqi's magic jelly beans."

Kojo was one of only three people who knew about Jake and the jelly beans. Their friend Grace Garcia was another. The third was Haazim Farooqi, the Ingestible Knowledge capsules' creator.

"To safely break the beams," said Jake, "I'm gonna need to break these first."

He pulled the binoculars out of his go bag and smashed them against the floor.

"Ouch," said Kojo. "Let's hope they don't charge us for that."

Jake reached into the cracked-open binoculars and removed one of the prisms between the eyepieces and the lenses. "The prisms are what turn the image right side up."

"I know," said Kojo. "We studied prisms in seventh grade. Back when you weren't paying attention to anything except video games."

Jake carefully lowered the prism into the path of one of the flickering lasers and, without breaking the beam, cautiously angled the glass until the pinpoint of light was deflected back to its source.

There was an electronic screech. The green beams disappeared. The laser had destroyed itself.

"MacGyver did that once," said Kojo. "I should've remembered."

"Who's MacGyver?" asked Jake as he positioned himself over the floor opening.

"Star of a 1980s TV show."

"Cool. What was it called?"

"*MacGyver*," said Kojo.

The two friends took turns lowering themselves down into the chamber. Lights automatically snapped on. They were in a ten-by-ten metal cube. Jake looked up and saw pipes overhead. *Those pipes have to be there for a reason,* he thought.

The pipes disappeared through the far wall with a stenciled 9 on it. That nine was above the spray-painted image of an equilateral triangle with three circles on each side. To the left of the triangle diagram were six small numbered circles.

"That's our next challenge," said Kojo.

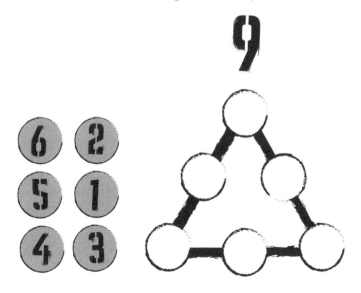

Jake went to the number circles and peeled one off the metal wall.

"They're rubbery magnets," he said.

"So what're we supposed to do?" asked Kojo, glancing at his wristwatch. "Because we better hurry up and do it. We're down to four minutes!"

"Professor Garcia gave me a puzzle like this during those IQ tests he ran on me."

Professor Garcia was Grace's father. He and his colleagues at Warwick College had certified Jake's IQ at "well in excess of three hundred." They'd been the first ones to call him "the smartest kid in the universe."

Jake tapped the stenciled 9 on the wall.

"We have to arrange the six number magnets along the legs of this triangle so each side adds up to nine."

"So why don't you go ahead and do that?" suggested Kojo. "Have I mentioned?" He showed Jake his wristwatch. "WE'RE RUNNING OUT OF TIME!"

4

Jake did some quick calculations.

It took him about ten seconds to slap all the round magnets onto their correct circles. Each of the three sides added up to nine.

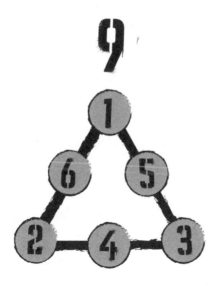

SWOOSH!

The metal wall slid sideways.

"There it is!" said Jake.

He gestured toward a glass box on the far side of the new room that had just opened up to them. Inside the wall-mounted display case was a glowing green orb the size of a softball. "That's the package the Consortium wants us to secure!"

Jake heard the steady *plink, plink, plink* of a drip.

He looked up.

Those ceiling pipes converged directly above the item they were supposed to retrieve. That was where the leak was.

It would be impossible to remove the glowing green orb without getting splashed by whatever was seeping out of the line directly above it.

"Hang on," said Kojo, sniffing the air in the new room. "You smell something?"

Jake sniffed. "Rotten eggs." He gestured up at the leak. "That could be sulfuric acid. Don't let it touch your skin. Or your eyes."

"I know," said Kojo. "Sulfuric acid can cause burns, blindness, irreversible organ damage, and possibly death. It's worse than those prescription-drug commercials my grandma watches."

"We have to stop the leak," said Jake. "Otherwise, we won't be able to complete our mission."

"Uh-oh," said Kojo. "The orb just turned yellow." He

checked his watch. "We're down to two minutes, baby. What are we supposed to do?"

How can you safely plug a sulfuric-acid leak? thought Jake.

He ran through all the math and physics and chemistry and plumbing stuff crammed inside his brain.

He got nothing.

This was so weird. Ever since he'd eaten Mr. Farooqi's Ingestible Knowledge capsules, almost every time he'd needed an answer it had been there, just waiting for him.

But now?!

Had he hit a mental wall? A dead zone in his brain? Was this one chunk of knowledge he hadn't ingested?

Or, worse, were the jelly beans starting to wear off?

Jake's stomach felt queasy.

Was this the beginning of the end?

5

"Hey, Kojo?" said Jake, his voice a little shaky. "You ever wonder if a gift can become a curse?"

Kojo shot him a look. "You ever wonder if, maybe, you should think about that kind of stuff *later*?"

Jake sighed. "Remember how happy I was before I got smart all of a sudden? When I was just me?"

" 'You' is all we need, baby. Just figure out how to plug that leak!"

"I can't."

"What?"

"I don't know what to do!"

Kojo snapped his fingers. "*MacGyver*!"

He tore open his gear bag and pulled out his second chocolate bar.

"One time, MacGyver plugged a sulfuric-acid drip with chocolate!"

Suddenly, something clicked in Jake's head.

"Of course. The sugar, or glucose, in the candy bar will react with the acid to generate an exothermic reaction, resulting in a thick, gummy putty. It'll block those holes!"

Jake and Kojo both unwrapped chocolate bars and carefully touched the edges to the acid leaks.

In seconds, the dripping stopped.

It worked!

Jake snatched the orb, which had just turned orange on its way to red.

A buzzer sounded. High-power exhaust fans whooshed to life.

"We did it!" shouted Kojo. "We beat the clock."

All four walls of the room slid sideways, exposing a high-tech underground lab. Several scientists in long white lab coats made notes regarding Jake and Kojo's performance in the drill.

"Bravo!" said Dr. Marie Doublé, head of the Consortium. "Bien joué!" She had a very thick French accent and always wore a fashionable silk scarf and jumbo ant-eye sunglasses.

"What'd she say?" Kojo whispered to Jake, because Kojo didn't speak French and Jake could speak twenty-seven different languages.

" 'Way to go,' " Jake whispered back.

"Oh. Okay. That's cool. And that's a wrap for me." Kojo handed his gear bag to the closest lab technician.

"For the record, my binoculars are the ones that *aren't* busted open. Come on, Jake. We need to head back to the mainland. Summer's almost over. It's time for a real vacation."

Jake nodded.

That had been the plan.

Run field tests for the Consortium and Dr. Doublé. Prove he would be a reliable and valuable asset for any upcoming super-secret international intelligence missions.

Then take the rest of the summer off. Go to Disney World with his mom and little sister, Emma.

But that was before Jake had started doubting himself and his so-called superpowers.

Was he really reliable and valuable?

Were the jelly beans still working?

Or was he on his way back to just being Jake McQuade?

6

"You performed quite well, Mr. McQuade," said Dr. Doublé as she drove Jake and Kojo in a gleaming golf cart down a brightly lit tunnel.

They were returning to the mainland underground.

"How about that chocolate-bar move with the acid drip?" said Kojo. "I came up with that one."

"Very clever," said Dr. Doublé. "It was, of course, the solution we hoped you would arrive at. It is why chocolate bars were included in your gear bag."

"Good thing I watch old *MacGyver* reruns," said Kojo. "Am I right?"

"Indeed you are. We had assumed that Mr. McQuade would've figured it out for himself."

Jake could tell: Dr. Doublé was questioning his genius superpowers almost as much as he was.

The golf cart came to a stop at the dead end of the very long, very sterile hallway.

Dr. Doublé pressed her palm to the white wall. A section rolled sideways to reveal a high-tech elevator. They all stepped aboard.

"By the way," said Kojo as the elevator whirred up its shaft, "Jake had to smash open his binoculars to beat those lasers. We didn't give you a damage deposit, did we?"

Dr. Doublé laughed. "No."

Kojo nodded knowingly. "And this is why. Sometimes you gotta break a few eggs to make an omelet."

"Or a roasted-red-pepper frittata," added Jake. "Or eggs en cocotte. Or an egg-in-a-hole sandwich with bacon and cheddar."

One of Mr. Farooqi's jelly beans had made Jake a gourmet chef who knew way too many ways to cook eggs.

After the elevator's high-speed ascent, its doors whooshed open. Jake, Kojo, and Dr. Doublé stepped out of the "supply closet" in the fake dental office that served as the Consortium's cover.

Dr. Doublé consulted her phone. "Your families are on the way and should be arriving shortly. We thank you both for agreeing to these field tests, and we look forward to working with you in the future."

Was she lying? Had Jake actually failed the Consortium's tests? Did the fact that Kojo was the one who'd figured out the answer to the sulfuric-acid problem lower his score?

"I'm going to my family's reunion in Georgia," said Kojo. "Two weeks of cousins, fun, and food, then—boom. It's back to school. But that's cool. Jake and I are going into the eighth grade. We will rule Riverview Middle School."

"And how about you, Jake?" asked Dr. Doublé. "Where will you be going with your mother and sister?"

"Florida," Jake said glumly. "Disney World." That came out sounding even gloomier.

"Um, that's supposed to be the happiest place on earth," said Kojo.

"You're thinking of Disney*land* in California," said Jake. "That's 'the happiest place on earth.' Disney *World* in Florida is 'the most magical place on earth.'"

"Riiiiight," said Kojo, because Jake didn't seem very magical *or* happy. "You okay, man?"

Jake turned to Dr. Doublé. "I want to keep working with you guys. Run a few more tests." Sure, he'd hate to miss his vacation, but he just had to know what was going on. Would he discover more dead zones in his brain?

"I suppose that could be arranged. . . ."

"Please?"

"Très bien," she said. "If you insist. When your mother arrives, please advise her of your decision."

"I will," said Jake. "Oh. I also need to go see Haazim Farooqi."

"And who is this Haazim Farooqi?" asked Dr. Doublé.

"Friend," said Kojo while Jake said, "Coach."

"He's a friendly coach," said Kojo.

"He always knows how to help me be my best," added Jake.

"He's like a sports psychologist," added Kojo. "Except without psychology. And not for sports."

"Very well," said Dr. Doublé. "We will arrange your transportation. Where exactly is Mr. Farooqi?"

"At Zinkle Inkle," said Jake.

"It used to be called Zinkle, Inc.," said Kojo. "But I told the new people in charge to change it. Zinkle Inkle has more pizzazz, know what I mean?"

Dr. Doublé's smile broadened. "Oui."

"That means 'yes,' right?"

"Oui" was all she said.

But Jake had a funny feeling Dr. Doublé might be hiding something.

7

Jake and Kojo were in the parking lot of the strip mall where Sunny Smiles Dental had its office.

"You're really going to stay here?" Kojo asked while they waited for his parents to arrive.

"Yeah. I want to make sure I still have what it takes."

"Uh-huh. In other words, you're still afraid your jelly beans are wearing off. That you're gonna lose your superpowers. I keep telling you, Jake, you're like Spider-Man. He only got bitten once by one radioactive spider. You ate what? Four dozen jelly beans?"

"Something like that."

"You aren't losing anything. Except maybe your ability to have a good time. You should slow your roll. Enjoy the ride."

Kojo's family pulled into the parking lot.

Jake helped load up Kojo's suitcases and gear and said his goodbyes to the Sheltons.

About ten minutes later, Jake's mom and his little sister, Emma, pulled up in their compact SUV.

Emma was three years younger than Jake and, in two weeks, would be going into the fifth grade at her Spanish-immersion elementary school.

"Where's your suitcase?" Jake's mother asked when she saw him standing empty-handed in front of the dentist's office.

Jake nudged his head at the window decal of the smiley-face tooth scrubbing its head with a foamy brush. "I, uh, need to stay a little longer. I might need . . ." He looked around to make sure no one was listening, then waggled his eyebrows to let his mom know he would be speaking in code. "A retainer for my overbite."

His mother rolled her eyes. She was sooo over talking in code.

"Well, I need a vacation," she said.

"Me too," pouted Emma.

"You guys go without me," said Jake. "Dr. Doublé and all the other, uh, orthodontists will keep an eye on me. I've got everything I need at the hotel. Food. Laundry. Wi-Fi."

"Are you sure?" asked his mom. "We'll miss you."

"I'll miss you guys, too. But . . ." He lowered his voice. "The world needs me, Mom."

"I know, I know," she said with a resigned sigh. "We'll be back in two weeks. Love you, hon."

"Love you, too," said Jake. "Here, Emma." He reached into his pocket and dug out a folded-over stack of bills. "This was going to be my vacation money. I want you to have it."

Emma's eyeballs nearly exploded.

"Really? All that money's for me?"

"Yep. Two hundred bucks. But you have to spend it all on vacation stuff like ice cream, a snorkel, and comic books."

Emma jumped up to give Jake a kiss.

"Oh, I almost forgot." Now Emma was the one digging into a pocket. "A sweet old lady at the grocery store heard that I was the smartest kid in the universe's sister and asked me to give you this."

Emma kept hunting in her pocket.

"I think she saw you on TV," their mom explained. "After that whole Genius Camp thing."

"Found it!" announced Emma. "I think it's funny."

She handed a small tin button to Jake. It said, *I enjoy bacon periodically,* only the word *bacon* was spelled with symbols from the periodic table of elements: Ba (barium), Co (cobalt), and N (nitrogen).

Jake smiled.

"You're right, Emma," he said. "It *is* funny!"

8

"Come along, Hubert!" snapped the boy's grandmother in her crisp British accent. "Get amongst it, you lazy lummox. Our target is on the move!"

"Yes, Grandmama," whined Hubert Huxley.

"Don't be such a weak-kneed whinger, Hubert! Your father was right. You'll never amount to anything. You don't have the fire in your belly."

"Are you experiencing indigestion again, Grandmama?"

"Oh, never mind. Spit-spot. Chauncy is waiting with the car." She glared at her phone. It was open to a tracking app. "This blinking dot is Jake McQuade. The rubbishy young man who outsmarted you at the Quiz Bowl."

"I know, Grandmama. I was there."

"Then he and his two friends also outsmarted your father *and* your cousin Patricia! Little brats!"

Hubert sighed. "I know all about that as well."

"Oh, quit your sighing. It's worse than your whining."

Hubert's grandmother's wrinkled face was permanently puckered into a scowl. Not just because she was angry at almost everything almost all the time, which she was, but also because both her late husband and then her son (Hubert's father) had extremely foul breath. The worst any creature on earth has ever exhaled, including dogs who eat horse poop. And so Penelope Flippington Huxley had resting stink face.

Her grandson Hubert was tall and lanky. At six feet six inches, he'd towered over all the other seventh graders at Sunny Brook Middle School and was the star of their basketball team. He also had a swoop of thick hair that he liked to stroke backward to make himself look more like the Joker from the Batman comic books. Hubert always liked the supervillains better than the ridiculous superheroes.

When his father was arrested and sent to prison for attempted murder, Hubert had to move in with his grandmama. That meant he wouldn't be attending Sunny Brook this year. Her multimillion-dollar penthouse apartment was in a different school district, close to the river. In two weeks, Hubert would be going into the eighth grade at Riverview Middle—the school where his cousin, Patricia Malvolio, had been the principal.

The six-story-tall school building was directly across the street from his grandmother's apartment. It was also the same school attended by Jake McQuade, Kojo Shelton, and Grace Garcia, the wretched, troublemaking threesome that had helped send Hubert's father and cousin to jail.

Hubert and his grandmother rode the elevator down to the lobby.

"Good morning, Mrs. Huxley," said the uniformed doorman.

"Says who?" she snarled back.

At the curb, Chauncy, the chauffeur, who, Hubert knew, had a very checkered past (something about driving getaway cars for bank robbers), opened the rear door of Grandmama's Rolls-Royce Phantom limousine.

Hubert helped his grandmother into the back seat and lumbered around to the other side to fold himself into the car.

His grandmother scrolled up the privacy screen so Chauncy couldn't hear what she said next.

She held up her phone and tapped the blinking red dot on the tracker app.

"This Jake McQuade is the reason you and I are so miserable. He helped that Grace Garcia steal our family's fortune!"

"But, Grandmama, the judge said it was *their* family's fortune."

"Only because, centuries ago, *their* ancestor, an insignificant little cabin boy, stole it from *our* ancestor, the noble Aliento de Perro."

Hubert nodded. He knew all about Capitán Dog Breath. And the mutiny. And how Dog Breath had stolen the *Stinky Dog*'s treasure from the cabin boy's father, who used to be the *Stinky Dog*'s captain.

There was a lot of backstabbing in pirate days.

Some of it with sabers.

Long story short, when Jake and his friends found the pirate treasure, Grace Garcia's family got all the booty. Hubert's father got fifteen to twenty-five years at New York's Sing Sing Correctional Facility. His cousin, Mrs. Patricia Malvolio, was serving her ten-to-fifteen-year term at the Bedford Hills Correctional Facility for women.

"But how did he do it?" seethed Hubert's grandmother.

"Pardon?"

"I hired private investigators. Dug into Jake McQuade's past. How did a slacker suddenly become brilliant? How could he become clever enough to steal what was rightfully ours?"

Hubert thought about that for a moment.

"Excellent questions, Grandmama," he said. "When I

first met McQuade, I must say he struck me as quite the dullard. He was only interested in playing mind-numbing video games. So how *did* he defeat my Quiz Bowl team, my father, Cousin Patricia, *and* the tech mogul Zane Zinkle?"

"A very interesting question, Hubert." His grand-mother's eyes were glued to the screen of her phone. "Especially since it seems young Mr. McQuade is on his way back to Zinkle headquarters even as we speak."

"What might he be doing there?" said Hubert.

"We'll soon find out."

Hubert's grandmother toggled the volume controls of her phone to make the sound louder.

"So, Frankie?" they heard a young voice say.

"Yeah?" said a gruffer, older voice.

"Would you rather own a horse the size of a cat or a cat the size of a mouse?"

"That's McQuade!" said Hubert.

"Of course it's him," snapped his grandmother. "The unsuspecting nincompoop is wearing a sophisticated tracking device disguised as a humorous lapel button. I gave it to his little sister when I accidentally-on-purpose bumped into her at the grocery store. It seems the child did exactly what I told her to do. She gifted the button to her big brother. Now, Hubert, you must do *your* job."

"Of course, Grandmama. But, if I may, what, exactly, is my job?"

"To observe Mr. McQuade."

She opened her clutch purse and pulled out an earbud.

"To find out how he became so 'brilliant.' Expose him, Hubert! For we must have our revenge, Hubert. We must do whatever it takes. We must find a way to destroy the boy who destroyed our family!"

9

"I think I'd go with the horse the size of a cat," said Jake's driver, Frankie, after thinking about it for a minute. "It'd be cute. Like a pony."

Frankie, a former Navy SEAL, was a member of what the Consortium called its "implementation team." In other words, he was part of their "muscle."

They pulled up to the guardhouse at the bridge leading to Zinkle's enormous corporate headquarters. The massive, four-story-tall smoky-glass building stood behind high-security fencing and a moat in the secluded, forested suburbs thirty minutes north of New York City. This woodsy corporate campus was where Jake and Kojo had gone to Genius Camp and defeated the company's billionaire founder and former whiz kid, Zane Zinkle.

"Huh," said Frankie, looking up into the rearview mirror.

"What?" said Jake.

"That car that just pulled into the visitor parking lot there. That's a Rolls-Royce Phantom. You don't see too many of those on the road."

"Because," said Jake, "the manufacturer's suggested retail price is four hundred and fifty-five thousand dollars. You have to be enormously wealthy to own one."

A worrisome thought flitted through Jake's anxious brain.

Who can afford such a fancy car?

Who besides Zane Zinkle?

The genius inventor (his IQ was below Jake's but probably above everybody else's) had escaped after Jake, Kojo, and Grace defeated him. He probably had a ton of money stashed in secret offshore bank accounts. Enough to buy a Rolls-Royce Phantom.

Enough to wreak revenge on Jake!

"We, uh, should head inside," said Jake. "Mr. Farooqi is waiting for me. And he's eager to start his summer vacation." The security guard raised the gate to the moat bridge.

They drove across the span.

Fortunately, the Rolls-Royce didn't follow.

10

"Greetings, Subject One!" said Mr. Farooqi when Jake stepped into Farooqi's spacious, high-tech laboratory. "We've come a long way from the basement of Corey Hall at Warwick College, haven't we, my friend? There my lab assistants were mice and a cockroach named Joe. Here? Everything is so shiny and new! Even my safety goggles. They are shiny and new, too!"

Farooqi was a bundle of eager energy. He had the wildly messy hair of most absentminded professors, which he wasn't. Well, he was absentminded. But he wasn't a professor. Not yet, anyhow. He was still working on his PhD.

His fully outfitted new lab was courtesy of Jake McQuade. Once Zane Zinkle had fled, Jake had worked out a deal with the new management team at Zinkle Inkle guaranteeing that Haazim Farooqi would always have a home for his research and experiments. Because scientists like Haazim Farooqi, the ones with big, seemingly impossible ideas, were just what the world needed.

Jake took in the glistening, sterile surroundings.

And, when Farooqi wasn't looking, he tossed the "bacon" button Emma had given him into a trash bin.

Mr. Farooqi was from Pakistan. And, like many Muslims, he never ate pork. The last thing Jake McQuade wanted to do was to offend the genius who had made him a genius.

"Look at this, Subject One!" said Farooqi, hugging a big beige box. "It is a microbiological quality-control NMR analyzer! It has blinking lights! See how they flicker? It cost over fifty thousand dollars! Ka-ching!"

Farooqi was giddy. A kid in a candy store.

"I've got beakers, beaker tongs, pipettes, spatulas, scoopulas, Erlenmeyer flasks, Florence flasks, any flask I could ask for!"

Farooqi's intense brown eyes looked even more intense when magnified by the wraparound safety goggles he wore because sometimes he forgot to turn down the blue flame on his Bunsen burners, which sometimes caused burbling glass beakers to explode and shatter.

Farooqi had come to the United States to study biochemistry with a focus on neurology, the study of the brain. He was only thirty-three and had already cracked the code for Ingestible Knowledge (IK).

Jake had inadvertently sampled Farooqi's first batch

of IK capsules in the form of jelly beans (okay, he ate them all) before Farooqi could pass them along to an eminent futurist lecturing at the Imperial Marquis Hotel, where Jake's mother worked. The renowned speaker had predicted that Ingestible Knowledge would be the "next big thing" in twenty or thirty years.

Farooqi wanted to show him that the world didn't need to wait that long.

But Jake found Farooqi's jar of IK capsules when he and Emma went to the hotel to mooch a free meal. The busy kitchen staff told Jake he'd have to wait.

Jake said okay.

But he was super hungry.

He saw the jelly beans sitting right there on a table in a glass jar.

They weren't labeled with anybody's name.

No one was around to claim them.

So he scarfed down the whole jar.

Less than half an hour later, he was super intelligent.

Only Farooqi, Kojo, and Grace knew the truth of how Jake McQuade had become the smartest kid in the universe.

"This must remain our secret until I am able to replicate my initial formulation," Farooqi always insisted.

He did make one new batch of beans that helped Jake restore some of the damage done by Zane Zinkle's brain-draining schemes. But Farooqi couldn't remember what he'd done. Not the first time *or* the second time.

He promised that, moving forward, he'd keep better notes.

"Oh dear!" Farooqi suddenly said. "I forgot to remind myself to pack something I am quite certain I will need on my vacation. I forget what it is. Perhaps my snorkel? Emergency underpants? I should've jotted it down!"

Jake shook his head. It looked like Mr. Farooqi was still keeping notes the same way.

Totally forgetting to do it.

And Jake's whole future as a brainy superhero might depend on Farooqi being able to recreate his IK formula.

Because without the jelly beans, Jake was nothing.

11

Hubert's grandmama snored.

Loudly.

She was napping in the sunny comfort of the Rolls-Royce, still parked in the visitor lot of the Zinkle campus.

Chauncy had lowered the brim of his chauffeur cap. He was asleep, too. Hubert imagined Chauncy could sleep anywhere. A skill that must've come in handy during his days as a getaway driver.

Hubert pressed the listening device deeper into his ear. McQuade was inside the corporate headquarters, talking to a Mr. Farooqi, first name Haazim.

It was hard to make out exactly what McQuade and Farooqi were talking about. The sound was muffled. Almost as if the device might be stuck inside some sort of wave-reflecting echo chamber. At times the voices were distant. Unintelligible.

But now they grew louder. McQuade and Farooqi must've moved closer to the miniature transmitter.

"Yes," Hubert heard Farooqi say. "I have, once again, replicated the KI formula."

"KI?" said McQuade.

"Security measures, my friend," said the scientist. "*IK* was too easy to decode. Everybody who saw those two letters would go, 'Oh, that must mean Ingestible Knowledge.'"

Hubert's mouth fell open.

Ingestible Knowledge?

Was that McQuade's secret?

"Then there's my website, beans4brains.net," Farooqi continued. "It is still under construction, but I do indeed define *IK* as 'Ingestible Knowledge.' My bad. But *KI*? Sure, it could stand for 'Knowledge Ingestible.' But it could also be short for 'Kidney-beanish Items,' since the capsules are very kidney-beanish, would you not agree, Subject One?"

Hubert sat up straight in his seat.

Subject One?

Was Jake McQuade part of some secret scientific study being done by Zinkle's company to enhance human intelligence? Was Zinkle trying to turn humans into computers, too?

"Is this new batch made with the same formula as the first two?" he heard McQuade ask.

"The same?" scoffed Farooqi. "Why on earth would I do that? Been there, done that, got the T-shirt. I will not be limited by anyone's preconceived perceptions of precision, Subject One. I follow my heart."

"Um, shouldn't you follow the science?"

"Oh, I do. But breakthroughs only happen when we break through a few rules. So I improvise. My KI may not be *exactly* the same as my IK, but it might also be *better,* for I have brought much passion to the project. That is why the purple ones now taste like passion fruit!"

Hubert heard the *clickety-clack* of hard-shelled pellets rattling against glass.

"Where are you taking that jar?" asked McQuade.

"Home. I will be gone for fourteen days. Two whole weeks! I don't want anyone here to tamper with my latest and greatest samples. We will run more tests when I return from my well-deserved holiday."

"Deal," said McQuade. "I need to do some more, uh, work. With the dentists."

"Ah yes," said Farooqi knowingly. "Dental hygiene is very important."

"Humans have thirty-two teeth," said McQuade. "Pigs have forty-four."

Hubert heard someone knocking on a door.

"Excuse me, Professor Farooqi?" said a new voice.

"Ah, hello, Christopher. This is my friend, Jake McQuade. He is here to wish me bon voyage, for I am going on vacation to Branson, Missouri. It will be my first rodeo!"

"Sounds like fun," said the new voice. It was louder than the others. "I'm just here to empty your recycling bin."

Hubert heard a thump and a clatter, a clink and a crunch.

The sound in his ear cut out.

Grandmama's sophisticated listening device had, apparently, just been crushed by the bottles and cans in Professor Farooqi's recycling bin. McQuade must've taken it off and tossed it away.

But that didn't matter.

Hubert had a pretty good idea of how Jake McQuade had become super intelligent super fast.

Ingestible Knowledge capsules!

Was such a thing really possible?

There was only one way to find out.

Hubert had to visit Haazim Farooqi's house while the professor was away on his vacation. He'd do a Google search. Find the address.

How convenient that the scientist would be out of town for two whole weeks! Hubert would learn how to thwart any and all home security systems. He'd break in and steal the "KI" capsules.

And he wouldn't tell his grandmother what he was up to until he discovered the truth. That Jake McQuade was an artificially intelligent phony and a fraud.

Hubert Huxley would prove it.

12

Two weeks later, after doing more top-secret training with Dr. Doublé and the Consortium, Jake headed back to Riverview Middle with Kojo.

"We are now officially eighth graders!" said Kojo triumphantly. "The top dogs. The big cheeses *and* the big enchiladas, which I hope they're serving for lunch today. I could really go for somethin' cheesy. . . ."

Mr. Charley Lyons, the principal, was standing in the lobby with Grace Garcia, who, like Kojo, was one of the top students in the school.

Grace was also the nicest girl at Riverview. At least that's what Jake thought, even though he was too chicken to tell her. Mr. Farooqi still hadn't come up with a jelly bean for talking to girls.

"Hi, guys!" Grace waved at Jake and Kojo. As usual, she was wearing an awesome pair of sneakers. Today she'd gone with her Hi-Vis Iridescent Chuck Taylor high-tops. Tomorrow? Who knew. Maybe neon Air Force Ones.

When Grace, Kojo, and Jake dug up Grace's family fortune, she and "Uncle Charley" (they were distantly related, even though Principal Lyons's family had left Cuba almost two centuries before Grace's family did) both became super rich. They donated most of their windfall to charities and to fixing up the school. They even put a ten-thousand-gallon wooden water tank up on the roof to improve the school's water pressure. But Grace kept enough cash on hand to fill her shoe closet with the world's coolest kicks. Yes. She had a whole closet for her sneaker collection.

She was also going to buy a Tesla when she got her driver's license.

"Thanks again for doing such a great job on the security system, Jake!" said Grace, gesturing at a small jewelry display in front of the school's trophy case. "You guys just missed the Channel Four news crew. They're doing a story about Eduardo Leones and the Red Lion!"

Inside the unbreakable cube on top of a sleek pedestal was the Leones Red Lion Diamond, one of the hundreds of precious jewels stashed inside the pirate treasure chest the three friends had uncovered. This one, the world's largest naturally colored "fancy red" diamond, weighed 5.2 carats and was graded as flawless.

It was also worth nearly eight million dollars.

It had been Principal Lyons's idea to keep one jewel

on display in the school lobby to remind everybody why Riverview Middle, which had been the most dilapidated school building in the district, now looked so magnificent. The brave cabin boy Eduardo Leones's booty had paid for everything!

Of course, keeping an eight-million-dollar diamond on display alongside the school's basketball, baseball, and Quiz Bowl trophies was a high-risk proposition.

Except that Jake McQuade, the smartest kid in the universe, had designed its showcase.

The cube was made out of glass-clad polycarbonate so thick it was "sledgehammer-proof." The pedestal was attached by high-strength bolts to a steel I beam hidden beneath the floor. Jake had engineered an incredibly sophisticated security system with tilt alarm, chip-key blocking, and an encrypted code that no one could crack unless, somehow, they had an IQ higher than Jake McQuade's.

"It looks great, Mr. Lyons," Jake told the principal.

"Thanks. Ah, here comes our new transfer student."

Jake bristled a little when he saw the six-foot-six giant striding through the front doors.

Because, even though it was only the first day of school, Jake already had serious issues with the new kid.

13

It was Hubert Huxley.

And, like always, there was a smug grin plastered on his face.

Jake remembered Hubert. From the basketball court. And the Quiz Bowl. And from when Hubert had tried to help his cousin, Riverview's former principal, sabotage the Riverview Quiz Bowl team.

"Welcome, Mr. Huxley," said Principal Lyons. "We're very excited that you'll be joining us this year."

"Indeed?" said Hubert, sounding as snobby as Jake remembered. He flicked a stray clump of his flouncy hair out of his eyes. "Rest assured, Mr. Lyons, the feeling is in no way mutual. I belong at Sunny Brook, a far superior school. Unfortunately, due to the actions of you four, my matriculation there is no longer an option."

He scowled at the diamond in the display case.

"Is that one of the gemstones your ancestor stole from my ancestor?"

"Actually," said Mr. Lyons with a very diplomatic chuckle, "as was established in court, Hubert, your ancestor stole the pirate ship and its treasure from Eduardo Leones's father, the rightful captain of the ship."

"Besides, baby," said Kojo, "we found the treasure before anybody in your family did. I believe the judge also cited the legal doctrine known as 'finderus keeperus, loserus weeperus.'"

"You stole what was rightfully mine. I shall never forget your vile actions. Nor shall I ever forgive them."

"So," said Jake, "does that mean you won't be trying out for the basketball team?"

"Ha!" Hubert laughed. "Ha, ha, ha."

Jake, Kojo, Grace, and Mr. Lyons all took a half step backward and fanned the air. After all those ha-has, the lobby smelled like crusty gym socks stuffed with moldy cheese.

"Excuse me," said Hubert. "I don't want to be late for my first day of classes."

He strutted away, shaking his head.

"I kind of feel sorry for the guy," said Grace. "Our good fortune was his bad luck."

Suddenly, Jake's phone started to thrum and play the theme song from *The Twilight Zone*.

"Sorry," he said to Mr. Lyons. "I forgot to turn it off."

Mr. Lyons smiled. "A common first-day-back mistake, Jake."

"That's Mr. Farooqi's ringtone," said Kojo.

"This could be important," said Grace.

Mr. Lyons gave them all a curious look. He didn't know about Farooqi or the jelly beans.

"If it's truly important, Jake," he suggested, "please take the call outside."

"Yes, sir."

Jake hustled out of the building and tapped the answer icon on his screen.

"Hey there, Mr. Farooqi," he said. "How was your vacation?"

"Wonderful. Until I returned home. Then, boom, I wished I had never gone to Branson or even Missouri! Someone broke into my apartment, Subject One! The sample jar is empty. Someone stole all my new jelly beans!"

14

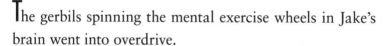

The gerbils spinning the mental exercise wheels in Jake's brain went into overdrive.

"Did they take anything else?" he asked.

"No," said Farooqi. "Not even the very stylish, clasp-lid storage jar that cost forty-five dollars. I suppose I was feeling festive when I made the purchase, for I had, once again, re-created my original creation. Or so we must assume. I never did any tests on the new batch."

"Did you call the police?"

"No. Not yet."

"That's probably smart."

"Well, Subject One," said Farooqi, sounding a little cranky, "if anybody would know 'smart,' it is you. Thanks, of course, to me."

Jake closed his eyes and rubbed them with his free hand. "What I mean is, how would you explain to the police that someone broke into your apartment and all they stole was a bunch of jelly beans?"

"Perhaps there is a notorious jelly bean thief on the prowl here in suburbia!"

"Who?" cracked Jake. "The Easter Bunny?"

"No, Subject One. The Easter Bunny would not be at the top of my list of suspects. If I understand things correctly, the Easter Bunny has plenty of jelly beans of his own. He grows them in fields of green cellophane grass."

Jake nodded. He needed a second to think.

Who would steal Farooqi's jelly beans?

Who even knew how valuable they were, besides Jake and his friends?

He might need some help investigating this theft. But who could he trust?

Jake had friends at the FBI. He'd helped the bureau's Deputy Assistant Director Don Struchen close a couple of tough cases. But how could Jake explain the significance of the missing jelly beans? The FBI would ask more questions than the police.

Kojo! Jake thought. He watched all sorts of old-school detective shows. Forensics was his hobby. In fact, he'd used some of his share of the pirate treasure money to buy a complete, professional-grade crime-scene investigation kit.

"Sit tight, Mr. Farooqi," said Jake. "Don't touch anything. Leave the crime scene exactly as you found it."

"With my socks scattered about on the floor?"

"Yes."

"What about my boxer shorts?"

"Those you can pick up. Kojo and I will be there as soon as we can."

"And when might that be? I need to go to the grocery store. Everything in the fridge has gone slightly green in my two-week absence."

"Today's the first day of school. So we can't be there until after three."

"I will wait."

Between periods, Jake explained the situation to Grace and Kojo. They huddled near a water fountain—the fancy kind where you could refill your bottle.

"Looks like we've got another mystery on our hands," said Kojo eagerly.

"Now you're quoting *Scooby-Doo* instead of *Kojak*?" said Grace.

"I'm doin' both, baby, because they're both classics."

"You guys?" said Jake. "Whoever stole the beans has to know what they really are."

"Or they just have a sweet tooth," said Kojo. "Hey, Jake—remember that time you punked me? You put frosting on that sponge and I thought it was a piece of cake. Chomped right into it. . . ."

"Kojo? Come on. This is serious!"

Kojo gave Jake a look. "You know what your problem is? You forgot how to have fun."

"Because with great power comes great responsibility, remember?"

"Doesn't mean you can't have a few laughs while you're taking care of business."

"Don't worry," Grace told Jake. "I'll hire you guys a car to take you up to Farooqi's."

"You still using that dude who charges for waiting time?"

"Yes."

"Then we better move fast!"

When the final bell rang, Jake and Kojo piled into the hired sedan waiting for them in the pickup lane.

First stop was Kojo's building. While he dashed inside to grab his detective equipment, Jake texted his mother.

> Something has come up. Kojo and I need to investigate.

With the FBI? his mom texted back.

No, Jake tapped in reply. Then he added: The Consortium.

Okay. It was a fib. But it would make the whole jelly

bean investigation sound more legit. As a rule, Jake never lied to his mother.

Except when it came to anything to do with the jelly beans.

She'd been so proud of everything Jake had accomplished since he became a certified genius.

He didn't want her to know the truth.

That he'd fooled the whole world.

That his newfound brainpower was all just AI.

Artificial intelligence.

15

"There is the jar!" said Farooqi, pointing to an empty container sitting on the pass-through from the living room to his kitchenette.

Farooqi's apartment didn't have much furniture. Just a recliner chair pointed at a TV. There was an empty pizza box on the floor.

"That yours?" asked Kojo, crouching down to examine the cardboard container.

"Yes," said Farooqi.

Kojo pried open the pizza box lid with a pencil.

Inside, he discovered a half dozen crusts and a splotchy grease stain.

"I had veggie pizza before I went on vacation," Farooqi explained.

Kojo nodded. "So the perp didn't bring the pizza with him. Interesting."

"He also didn't steal the TV set," said Jake.

"Stand back," said Kojo. "I need to dust that jelly bean jar for fingerprints."

He snapped open the aluminum attaché case with all his crime-scene-investigator gear tucked into tidy foam slots.

"I'm going with the fluorescent-dye stain technique," Kojo explained. "Regular dusting with aluminum flake could contaminate the evidence. Plus, it's not as much fun as this glow-in-the-dark stuff."

Kojo went to work.

Jake's eyes swept across the living room. Other than the chair, the TV, and the pizza box, there wasn't much to see. A crumpled foil bag of Chillz Chatpata potato sticks. An empty Shezan bottle. Both were popular snack choices in Pakistan.

"Not much in here for a thief to steal," he commented.

"You are correct, Subject One," said Farooqi. "My humble abode is quite desolate. But I am seldom here. I spend most of my time at the lab, working on my jelly beans."

"Which confirms that whoever broke into your apartment only came here looking for the IK capsules."

"KI," whispered Farooqi.

"Riiiight," said Jake.

Kojo snapped off his rubber gloves. "This job was done by a pro. There are zero prints on the jar."

Kojo went to the front door and examined its flimsy locks.

"You could break in here with a credit card," he said.

"Yes," said Farooqi. "I had to do that one night. I had left my keys in my other pants."

Kojo clasped his hands behind his back and paced around the nearly empty living room.

"So tell me, Mr. Farooqi—who at Zinkle Inkle knew what you were working on?"

"Nobody," said Farooqi. "Except, of course . . ."

He pointed an accusatory finger at Jake and Kojo.

"You two! Did you boys steal my jelly beans?"

"No," said Jake.

"Mr. Farooqi?" said Kojo. "Is there anybody at work who might be a suspect?"

Farooqi snapped his fingers.

"Jill Merkle!" he said. "I think she is the one who steals my yogurt out of the break-room refrigerator even though I write my name on the lid."

Kojo nodded knowingly. "And did this Jill Merkle see you walking out of the building with a jar of jelly beans?"

"No," said Farooqi. "I transported them home in my briefcase. Excuse me. I will show you."

He went into the bedroom and returned carrying a plastic shopping bag with handles.

"That's your briefcase?" said Jake.

"Yes. Has been for many years. It is indestructible and the handles are, as the name implies, quite handy."

He froze. Because he had pried open the top of the bag and seen something inside.

"Kamaal hai!" exclaimed Farooqi.

Joy filled his eyes.

"All is not lost, my young friends! One bean remains!"

16

Farooqi reached into the rumpled plastic shopping bag.

"This was hidden behind a pile of papers and another pair of socks! Behold—my only remaining KI capsule!"

He held up a speckled jelly bean pinched between his thumb and forefinger. He gave it a stiff sniff.

"Tutti-frutti," he announced.

"Which batch is that bean from?" asked Jake.

"The first. Or maybe the second. Could be the third."

"You can't tell?"

"No, Subject One. They are not labeled. Perhaps, in the future, I will give every single jelly bean its own miniature marking. Perhaps I could paint it on like the *m*'s on all those M&M's. Whose job is that, I wonder? They must have very good eyesight. The *m*'s are so tiny. . . ."

Jake let out a sigh. They were getting nowhere.

"Is there anything else?" he asked.

"Yes!" said Farooqi. "Thanks to this tutti-frutti bean, I can now do research to determine what it was I did in the first place! I can, once again, reverse-engineer my brilliant creation. Maybe. We'll see."

"How about footprints?" asked Kojo, trying to bring Farooqi's focus back to the crime scene. Kojo had been on his hands and knees, examining the living room rug with a magnifying glass. "Because I'm not seeing anything down here but your potato-stick crumbs."

"I noticed nothing out of the ordinary," said Farooqi. "Except a pair of gauzy shoe booties and a hairnet I found out in the hall when I first arrived home."

Kojo sprang up. "Where are they?"

"I threw them down the trash chute to the incinerator before I entered my apartment," said Farooqi. "The board of this condo complex frowns upon litter in the hallways. And since the items were right outside my door, I knew who would be held responsible for this infraction. Me!"

"That could've been evidence!" said Kojo.

"It was," said Jake. "Evidence that this break-in was done by a pro who knew how to get in, grab what they were looking for, and get out without leaving any sign that they were ever here."

"Except for that dumping-their-booties-in-the-hall business," said Kojo. "You ask me, that was a rookie mistake."

"True," said Jake. "But maybe they did that so we'd *think* they were an amateur."

"They also left a note," said Farooqi.

"What?!" said Jake and Kojo simultaneously.

"He or she—one mustn't make assumptions—left a note. On a small card."

"And you didn't think you should mention that?" said Kojo, tossing up both his hands.

"I did. But then I forgot to remember it."

Of course he did, thought Jake.

"What'd the note say?" he asked.

"Hang on." Farooqi reached into his shirt pocket and pulled out a small ivory business card.

"And now even more evidence is contaminated with *your* fingerprints," muttered an exasperated Kojo.

"I'm sure the card is clean," said Jake. "The jelly bean thief probably wore gloves when they wrote the note."

"No," said Farooqi. "I believe they printed it from their computer."

Kojo grabbed the card out of Farooqi's fingers with his CSI kit's stainless-steel forceps. "Comic Sans typeface," said Kojo, shaking his head in disappointment.

Jake nodded. "A very common, some would say overused, font. What does the message say?"

Kojo showed Jake the card:

```
I know your secret.
```

17

Zane Zinkle was streaming the New York City news while slurping ramen noodles from a microwavable plastic bowl.

The former head of Zinkle Inc.—maker of Zinkle computers, zPhones, zPads, zBox gaming systems, and multiple top-secret weapons systems—was holed up in his remote hideout: a secluded lakefront cabin in the Adirondack Mountains of upstate New York.

Zinkle, who was still a bazillionaire thanks to his secret bank accounts, had flown his personal escape pod the 260 miles from Zinkle headquarters to his well-stocked and fully wired hiding place. He'd had to flee the Zinkleplex after Jake McQuade, the so-called "smartest kid in the universe," had defeated Zinkle and his Virtuoso quantum computer.

A defeat that still stung.

Zane Zinkle used to be the "world's smartest child." He was even in the *Guinness World Records* book with that title. But then Jake McQuade came along. The young, freckle-faced fool had stolen Zinkle's crown!

Now the local news reporter at Channel 4 was mentioning McQuade's name again.

"This spectacular gemstone, currently on display near the trophy case of Riverview Middle School, is known as the Leones Red Lion Diamond. It was but one of the many precious jewels, gems, and artifacts stashed inside the treasure chest discovered by current eighth graders Grace Garcia, Kojo Shelton, and Jake McQuade. According to the school's principal, this diamond—which I'm told is protected by the world's most advanced high-tech security system—is on display to remind students that this school's shiny new future is all thanks to something that happened in the past, when the cabin boy on a pirate ship in what would become New York Harbor—"

Zinkle clicked the mute button on his computer. It was one of many such machines in his lair. His spacious and cozy cabin might have been remote, but it was well connected thanks to multiple secure satellite dishes. It also had a sauna and very nice bed linens.

Zinkle was dressed in his standard uniform: blue jeans and a black turtleneck. There were three dozen of each hanging in the cabin's cedar-lined closets. His bowl haircut still had bangs that looked like they'd been trimmed with a toenail clipper. But it was what was underneath that thinning hair that counted.

His magnificent brain!

Which was whirring. Because the TV news people had just confirmed that the rumored Red Lion Diamond was real. It was also exactly what Zinkle needed for his next big thing. Well, it was half of what he needed, but still. It was a start. No, it was a giant leap for Zinkle-kind. He adjusted his glasses with the tip of his pinky finger.

He hit a few keys on a secondary keyboard and turned to smile at the screen of computer number three. It was the device linked to the most secure of all his extremely secure communications interfaces.

It was time to make a video call to his contact and potential business partner.

With a few simple keystrokes, he made the connection.

"Monsieur Zinkle," said his business partner. "So good to see you. I trust you are well?"

Zinkle wasn't big on chitchat.

"I'll make this brief," he said. "The Red Lion Diamond. The one Mr. McQuade and his companions put on display at their middle school in New York City. It would work quite well in the device you want me to build for you. It won't give us *everything* we need. But it's an excellent first step. For the weapon to achieve its maximum potential, we'll need a second, even larger diamond. And not just any diamond. Oh no. I want that giant orange one I told you about. The flawless gemstone stolen over three hundred years ago from a ship sailing to England. A diamond no one has seen in centuries."

"Thank you for this information," said his contact. "Rest assured, we currently have full access to that other . . . *item* we discussed. The one you'd really like to get your hands on, so to speak."

"Excellent. You are keeping up your end of the bargain. Now go get me the two diamonds! We'll need both to reach our full potential."

On the monitor, Zinkle's mysterious contact promised to "facilitate the procurement of the precious jewels ASAP."

In other words, the hunt for the orange diamond would continue.

But the Red Lion would be stolen immediately.

18

Jake, Kojo, and Mr. Farooqi agreed not to call the police or the FBI or even Jake and Kojo's new friends at the Consortium. They didn't want anyone asking questions about the stolen jelly beans and why they were so important.

"Let's let the thief make the first move," coached Kojo. "We'll just make sure we make the last one!"

The next morning, while Kojo and Jake were walking to school, Jake said out loud what he'd been fearing inside.

"It has to be Zane Zinkle."

"That's what I'm thinking, too," said Kojo. "He strikes me as a Comic Sans kind of guy."

"When we were at Genius Camp, Zinkle told me he'd researched my 'academic history.'"

"You mean your lousy report cards?"

"Exactly. He knew that until I took Dr. Garcia's IQ

test, my only 'accolades' were my high scores on *Zombie Brain Quest*."

"So," said Kojo, "he's been tailing you. Tracking your every move. He somehow figured out your secret."

"How, though? Zinkle hasn't been seen in months. I know I haven't seen him."

"But he's still rich. He could hire people to hire people to follow you."

"All the way to Farooqi's lab."

Suddenly, Kojo stopped in his tracks.

"Wait a second. What if Zinkle *ate* the jelly beans? He's already a genius. What if he becomes a supergenius? What if he winds up even more geniusy than you?"

Jake looked sick to his stomach. "Welcome to my nightmare."

The two friends walked on in silence. Jake could smell the breeze coming off the Hudson River. Riverview Middle School had, as the name implied, an excellent view of the nearby Hudson River.

When they stepped into the lobby, they saw Grace over near the diamond display.

She was smiling and chatting with Hubert Huxley.

"I know how much it meant to you last year," Jake heard Grace say. "So, if you want to be on our Quiz Bowl team, we'd be happy to have you." She saw Jake and Kojo. "Wouldn't we, guys?"

"Maybe," said Kojo. "Depends. Lots of variables to take into consideration."

Grace laughed. "Look, everybody knows that Jake McQuade is, officially, the smartest kid in the universe. It wouldn't be fair to all the other schools in the district for him to stay on as the third member of our Quiz Bowl team."

"I agree," said Jake.

"So, Hubert, since you can't play for Sunny Brook, how'd you like to play for Riverview?"

Hubert snorted.

"No thank you, Miss Garcia. Your offer is chucklesome and risible."

Grace, Kojo, and Jake all gave Hubert a baffled look.

Jake had an inkling of what *risible* meant. But *chucklesome*? That vocabulary word wasn't in any of the jelly beans.

"Oh, I'm sorry," said Hubert. "Let me lower my lexicon to a level you three might grasp. Your offer, Miss Garcia, is ridiculous."

He turned on his heel and marched away.

"Nice guy," mumbled Kojo.

"It's not his fault," said Grace. "He's in a bad place."

"Really?" said Jake. "I thought you liked Riverview."

"I mean Hubert's in a bad personal space. His father's in prison. His cousin, Mrs. Malvolio, is behind bars, too. He has to live with his grandmother. I think we should cut him some slack."

"All right," muttered Kojo. "Fine. Slack shall be cut."

Grace looked up and down the hallway. Made certain no one was eavesdropping.

"Besides," she whispered. "I just learned something that'll be way more fun than obsessing over Hubert Huxley."

"What's up?" Jake whispered back.

"I'm pretty sure there's more pirate treasure!"

19

Grace led the way to the janitor's closet that used be her uncle Charley's office before he was promoted to principal.

Now it was just a storage room with shelves full of toilet paper and that parmesan-cheese-scented sawdust powder they dumped on puke puddles. The three friends had turned it into their secret clubhouse.

"We've got some time before the bell rings for homeroom," said Grace.

She swiped her thumb across the screen of her phone and brought up an album of photos.

"So, yesterday after school I heard from Lisa Schmidt Schroeder at Elite Antiques."

"The same Lisa Schmidt Schroeder who sold all the pirate booty?" asked Kojo.

"Yep. Anyway, she sent me her itemized log. A list of all the stuff she auctioned off. She added notes about each piece's unusual characteristics. Going through that list last night, I discovered a pattern."

"I like patterns," said Jake.

"This was a string of words that kept popping up on the list."

"And what were those words?" asked Jake.

"They had to do with the golden plates and goblets," said Grace. " 'Engraved on the bottom with blank.' "

Kojo raised both eyebrows. "Someone actually etched the word 'blank' on the bottom of all that fine dinner-ware?"

Grace laughed. "No. I just said 'blank' because every piece had a different word scratched into it." Grace swiped to a scanned image of a list of words she'd made. "These are those words."

hijos
calabaza.
Lo siento,
Esto
no
repugnante
le arrebató
es
todo.

El dragón
la gran
míos.

"It's Spanish," said Jake.

"¡Maravilloso!" said Grace.

"Wait a second," said Jake. "This is like those rocks we found in the cave. Where each one had a single word engraved on it."

"A single Spanish word!" said Kojo, remembering. "But we had to put them together in a way that made sense. That was before Jake studied Spanish. He put the stones together all wrong. Remember that, Jake? Remember when you totally messed up the stone sentence?"

"Yes, Kojo. I remember."

"Me too. Don't think I'll ever forget it."

"No. I don't think you ever will."

"So," said Grace, checking her watch, "I'll cut to the chase. I used the punctuation marks—the three periods, the comma—and the capital letters as cues. The periods had to come at the end of the sentences, the capital letters at their starts. I spent a whole bunch of time trying out different combinations. Went through several different possibilities. Thought about words that went together, those that didn't."

"And?" said Kojo and Jake, both rolling their hands

to urge Grace to hurry up, because she was supposed to be cutting to the chase.

"And," she said, sliding her thumb to a fresh image, "this is what I came up with."

Lo siento, hijos míos.
Esto no es todo.
El dragón repugnante le arrebató la gran calabaza.

Jake translated the three sentences in a flash.

" 'Sorry, my children. This is not everything. The foul dragon snatched the big pumpkin.' "

"Is this from some kind of ancient Spanish fairy tale?" asked Kojo. "In the Spanish version, did a dragon steal Cinderella's pumpkin carriage? Maybe breathe on it and steam it into a pumpkin spice latte?"

"Hardly," said Grace. " 'The foul dragon' is what the cabin boy, Eduardo Leones, might've called the mutineer who killed his father and took over the pirate ship known as the *Stinky Dog*."

"Captain Dog Breath," said Jake. "Hubert Huxley's ancestor. We heard all about him when the judge was ruling about whose family had the best claim to the treasure. But what is 'la gran calabaza'? What's 'the big pumpkin'?"

"I did some research," said Grace. "I'm pretty sure it's another diamond. A gigantic orange jewel. In fact, it might be the biggest diamond in history. They say it weighed three pounds. No one knows for sure, because no one has ever seen it. The Big Pumpkin was on a merchant ship headed for England that was boarded by pirates. Then *those* pirates lost it to another bunch of what they called 'foul-smelling, mad-dog' pirates."

"The *Stinky Dog*," said Kojo.

"That's what I'm thinking," said Grace. "Most people think the whole thing is just a legend. A made-up story."

"Would make a pretty good sea shanty," observed Kojo. He started singing. "There once was a ship that put to sea, and the captain's breath was very stink-y!"

"But," said Jake, "we know the truth. The *Stinky Dog* was a real pirate ship."

"And," added Grace, "if what I read about the Big Pumpkin is correct, if the diamond is real, it's worth a fortune."

"Can you define 'a fortune'?" said Kojo.

"Sure. This one ginormous diamond would be worth more than all the other pirate treasure we found. Combined!"

20

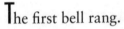

The first bell rang.

Jake, Kojo, and Grace walked up the hallway together, headed for class.

Jake figured he already had enough to worry about without becoming involved in another pirate treasure hunt.

Somebody had stolen Mr. Farooqi's new jelly beans.

And, most likely, that somebody was Zane Zinkle, who was off supercharging his already genius brain, taking it to a whole new level so he could wreak his revenge on Jake McQuade, the guy who'd stolen his crown as the world's most brilliant kid *and* knocked him off the throne at his high-tech empire. Did Jake really want to add "hunt for more pirate booty" to his crowded to-do list?

"I think the Big Pumpkin is cool," he said to Grace,

trying for a smooth exit. "But do we really need to find more treasure?"

"No," said Grace. "We don't *need* to do it. But it might be fun. Challenging."

"Totally," said Kojo. "I'm all in."

"Come on, Jake," said Grace. "Just think. The three of us, working a new puzzle. It'll be a blast."

"We could get the band back together and play our greatest hits," added Kojo.

Jake gave Kojo a double-eyebrow-raised look of concern.

"Oh, right," said Kojo, reading Jake's face. "There's that other thing."

"What other thing?" said Grace.

Jake nudged his head sideways. The three friends executed a swift U-turn and scurried back to the janitor's closet. The second bell was about to ring, so Jake had to make this fast.

"Somebody stole Mr. Farooqi's latest batch of jelly beans," he told Grace.

"You're kidding."

"I wish I was."

"We think it was Zane Zinkle," said Kojo. "We think he wants to come after Jake. Dude can hold a grudge."

"Jake, do you have any proof that you're in danger?" asked Grace. "If so, we should call the police and—"

"Tell them about Farooqi's jelly beans so we can ruin

his life along with mine?" Jake was being a little melodramatic. They were in a hurry. Melodrama sometimes sped things up.

"Okay, okay," said Grace. "I understand. But, come on, you're Jake McQuade. You're 'the smartest kid in the universe.' You can multitask. You can hunt for treasure *and* battle Zane Zinkle at the same time."

"Sure you can, baby," added Kojo.

And then Grace gave Jake her warmest smile. "We'd really appreciate it."

Jake's whole body felt like it was melting into a mushy pile of jiggly goop.

"Okay," he said, when he finally found his voice. "I'll, uh, multitask."

"Now we're talking," said Kojo.

The second bell rang. Jake, Kojo, and Grace bolted out of the closet.

They were all going to be late to class.

21

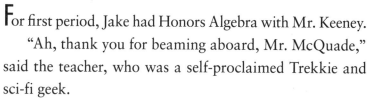

For first period, Jake had Honors Algebra with Mr. Keeney.

"Ah, thank you for beaming aboard, Mr. McQuade," said the teacher, who was a self-proclaimed Trekkie and sci-fi geek.

The T-shirts Mr. Keeney wore under his rumpled sports coat were always funny. Today's showed a right A-B-C triangle with a moose scaling the slope of the slanted A-C line. Because it was the "hypotemoose."

"Sorry," said Jake, slipping into his seat. "I, uh, had to take care of something."

"Was it a problem in search of a solution?"

"Yes, sir. Sort of."

"And did you find the answer?"

"Not yet."

"Well, let's hope you have better luck here in class."

He clicked his laptop. A logic puzzle appeared on the Smart Board at the front of the room.

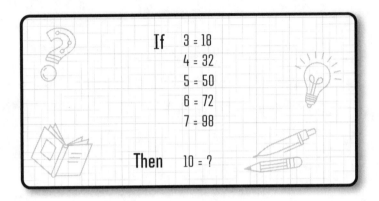

If   3 = 18
4 = 32
5 = 50
6 = 72
7 = 98

Then   10 = ?

Everybody in the classroom moaned (except, of course, Jake).

"Settle down, people," said Mr. Keeney. "This is today's warm-up drill. We need to get our brains fired up. Jake? Help 'em out."

Jake glanced at the puzzle. "Ten equals two hundred," he said.

"Correct," said Mr. Keeney. "Kindly show us your work."

"Um, okay," said Jake. "Three times six is eighteen. Four times eight is thirty-two. A pattern is established. We need to add two to the multiplying number each time we go up a number. So five times ten is fifty, and so forth, until we skip down to the last number, ten, where our multiplier would be twenty. Twenty times ten is two hundred."

"Huzzah," said Mr. Keeney. "Math is fun, people. It

teaches you valuable skills. Like if you're cold, head to the corner of a square, where it's always ninety degrees."

The whole class groaned.

"How about this one?"

Mr. Keeney moved on to the next slide.

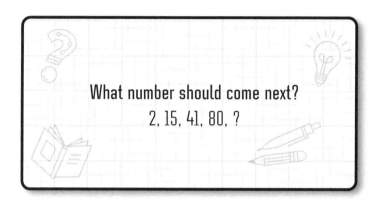

What number should come next?
2, 15, 41, 80, ?

"Anyone?"

Jake raised his hand.

"Anyone except Mr. McQuade. Yes. You in the back. The new guy." Mr. Keeney fumbled with his seating chart. "Mr., uh, Huxley. What's the answer?"

"One hundred and thirty-two."

"Correct. Care to explain how you arrived at your brilliant deduction?"

"I'd rather not," said Hubert. "If an answer's right, it's right. Proceed to the next problem."

"I'd really like to hear how—"

"And I'd really like to learn something that I don't already know, so let's move along, shall we?"

Mr. Keeney muttered something under his breath, then jabbed the forward arrow on his computer several times. He streamed through a series of challenging puzzles until he came to one that seemed to delight him.

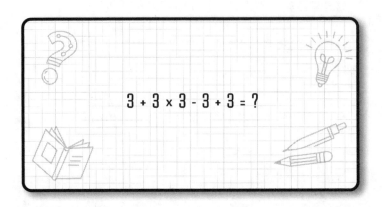

$$3 + 3 \times 3 - 3 + 3 = ?$$

"Ah, yes. How about this, Mr. Huxley," the teacher said with a sly grin. "Is *this* challenging enough for you?"

Hubert heaved a bored sigh. From the looks on their faces, his nearest neighbors smelled it.

"Maybe Jake can help you out." Mr. Keeney turned to him. "Mr. McQuade?"

Jake studied the screen.

It was pretty simple. Three plus three was six. Six times three was eighteen. Eighteen minus three was fifteen. Fifteen plus three was eighteen.

"I don't require McQuade's assistance," said Hubert. "And your devious attempt at trickery will not fool me, Mr. Keeney, for I know my order of operations. One must always do all multiplication and division before doing any addition or subtraction. Therefore, the answer you seek, and assumed I would not ascertain, is twelve."

"That is correct, Mr. Huxley," said Mr. Keeney without much enthusiasm.

Jake tried not to show it, but deep down he was freaking out.

He'd reached the wrong answer.

He'd thought it was eighteen, not twelve!

Was the algebraic order of operations located in a corner of his brain that the Ingestible Knowledge capsules had never reached?

Worse, was he right? Were his jelly beans wearing off?

"Well done, Mr. Huxley," said Mr. Keeney. He held up one hand and made a wide Vulcan *V*. "Live long and prosper."

Hubert smirked and gave Jake a sideways sneer.

"Oh, I intend to, Mr. Keeney. I definitely intend to."

22

During lunch, Jake told Grace and Kojo what happened in math class.

"I couldn't figure out the answer. It's like that math part of my brain was momentarily missing. Hubert Huxley nailed the answer right away."

"The jelly beans," whispered Kojo. "They're wearing off. Just like you always figured they would."

"You guys?" said Grace. "Don't jump to conclusions. It was just a hiccup. Of course Hubert figured out the answer. He's not under as much pressure as you, Jake. Plus, he's super smart. Remember how he and his team from Sunny Brook almost beat us in the first round of last year's Quiz Bowl?"

Jake realized Grace might be right. But still. The thought of the superintelligence from the jelly beans fading away haunted him.

"Grace?" said Jake. "Can I bother you for another limo ride? I need to visit Mr. Farooqi after school."

"What's up?"

"Tutti-frutti," said Kojo, as if it were the name of a top-secret mission.

"Luckily," Jake explained to Grace, "Mr. Farooqi has one bean left. We can analyze it. Run tests. See if obsolescence is baked into IK's cake."

"Maybe your jelly beans are past their sell-by date," said Kojo. "Like string cheese that's been in the back of the fridge too long."

Jake checked in with his mother on the ride up to Farooqi's lab.

"I should be home by seven," he told her.

"Make it seven-thirty," she said.

"Huh?"

"*Quiz Zone* comes on at seven, and it's more fun if you're not here answering everything before Emma and I even finish reading the clue."

Jake had to laugh. "Fine. Seven-thirty."

"So, Subject One," said Farooqi the second the lab door was shut behind Jake. "Have you found the jelly bean thief?"

85

"No. But we have a prime suspect."

"Aha! Just like at the murder-mystery dinner theater I like to attend on my nights off, which I have not had since you stole my first batch of jelly beans."

"I didn't steal—"

Farooqi flapped his hand to swat the thought away. "Water under the bridge, Subject One. Beavers over the dam. Let us proceed to the matter at hand." There was a pause. "What is the matter at hand? Why are you here?"

"I want to analyze that tutti-frutti jelly bean!"

"Aha. And, as intelligent as you are, you cannot do so without me, the father of the beans."

"Right," said Jake. He gestured around the cluttered lab. "We also probably need all this equipment."

"Which, might I remind you, only I know how to operate!"

"Exactly."

"Okey-dokey, then," said Mr. Farooqi. "Do not despair, Subject One." He held up the small speckled jelly bean, which was now sealed inside a tiny zip-top bag. "I will run every test imaginable on this KI capsule. And then I will think up some *un*imaginable ones and run those, too. Soon, thanks to the marvels of modern science, we will know everything there is to know about this last jelly bean, which, actually, might've been one of the first. I really need to clean out my plastic-bag briefcase more often."

Yeah, thought Jake. *You really do.*

And so they went to work. They ran tests. They did scans. They did spectrum analysis, gas chromatography, vitamin analysis, and impurities testing.

But there was still "much, much more to do," according to Mr. Farooqi.

"There are so many tests we must run," he said. "I'm afraid this could take days, maybe weeks!"

Shortly after seven, Jake's phone dinged.

Then it started buzzing.

It was Principal Lyons. He never called Jake.

"I have to take this," he told Farooqi.

"Sure, sure. I will continue the diligent pursuit of science while you chitchat with your chums."

Jake answered the call "Hello? Mr. Lyons? What's up?"

"I'm here at the school, Jake. With the police."

"The police? What happened?"

"Your brilliant security system worked. Someone tried to steal the diamond. But they couldn't crack your code. A silent alarm went directly to the precinct. A pair of uniformed officers got here in a flash."

"Did they catch the thief?"

"No. The would-be burglar had already fled the scene."

"What about the security cameras?"

"We have fantastic video images of someone wearing a spooky Halloween mask under a hoodie."

"Any fingerprints?"

"No. Whoever broke in was a real pro. They knew exactly what they were doing. How to get in and out without leaving any evidence that they were ever here."

Jake nodded.

A real pro.

Just like whoever stole Mr. Farooqi's jelly beans.

23

The evening after the attempted burglary at the school, Hubert and his grandmother were in her penthouse apartment watching *Quiz Zone* on TV.

The final question was always the hardest.

"What is the shortest word with the suffix -*ology*?" asked the host.

"*Oology*," said Hubert while, on the screen, the returning champion and her two competitors thought about their answers.

"*Oology?*" sneered his grandmama. "What on earth is that?"

"The study of bird eggs."

A buzzer sounded on the TV. "Sorry," said the host. "Time is up. We were looking for 'oology,' the study of bird eggs."

Hubert snapped the remote.

His grandmother gawped at him as if he were a creature from another planet.

"My, my, my," she said. "You're even smarter than I remembered."

Hubert shrugged but didn't say anything else.

"How old are you?" his grandmama asked.

"Twelve."

"And already your breath has turned."

"Excuse me?"

"The family halitosis." Her eyes were watery. "The 'dog breath,' if you will. It usually doesn't show up in male descendants of Aliento de Perro until they turn eighteen."

"Sorry if my breath offends you, Grandmama," said Hubert.

"Hardly. It tells me that you are . . . ready." She said it as if she expected thunder to crack when she did.

"Ready?" said Hubert. "For what?"

"Your destiny!" she declared. "Your quest. Your father grew distracted. So did your grandfather. They both took the easy way. Spent their energies searching for the second-place prize—the cabin boy's buried treasure chest."

"That was the *second-place* prize?" said Hubert cynically. "It was worth hundreds of millions of dollars. What, pray tell, does the first-place winner get?"

"¡La Gran Calabaza!"

"La what?"

"The Big Pumpkin!"

This time, thunder did boom.

Hubert ignored it. "Pumpkin?" he chuckled. "Why should anyone care about a big pumpkin? Halloween is still weeks away."

"I'm talking about the world's largest orange diamond, you ninny!" Her eyes grew wide and wild. "Whoever attempted to steal the Red Lion Diamond from that foolish school across the street should've set their sights higher. ¡La Gran Calabaza!"

No thunder this time, but Grandmama's face—illuminated from below by a table lamp—looked extremely craggy and creepy.

"It was stolen by the pirates of the *Stinky Dog* from another band of pirates who'd stolen it from a merchant ship on its way to England. La Gran Calabaza weighs three pounds!"

Hubert whistled. He knew that there were approximately 142 carats to an ounce. That meant the Big Pumpkin would weigh in at about 6,816 carats.

Hubert also knew—thanks to all the IK or KI capsules he'd recently ingested—that a 14.82-carat orange diamond had sold at auction in Geneva for twenty-one million dollars. The Big Pumpkin would be worth . . . multiply by the carats . . . put in the commas . . . over nine *billion* dollars!

Math was so much fun. Especially when it came to jumbo-sized diamonds.

"Before the British sailors seized him and shipped him

back to London," his grandmama continued, "your noble ancestor Capitán Aliento de Perro hid the giant diamond somewhere in New York Harbor. Your father's father told him all about it. This tale has been passed down for generations upon generations."

"Tell me more, Grandmama," said Hubert, rubbing his hands together. He'd like to be a pirate captain someday. Maybe a supervillain pirate captain.

His grandmother leaned in. "Captain Dog Breath's final visitor, the last person he spoke to before the prison chaplain arrived to escort him off to the gallows, was his son, to whom he gave a clue: 'las tres hermanas ostras.' "

"The three oyster sisters," said Hubert, who suddenly understood Spanish, a subject he'd never studied.

But who were these oyster sisters?

Fishmongers from the seventeenth century?

"That's the only clue the old geezer gave the fellow?" he asked his grandmother. "That's not much to go on."

His grandmother narrowed her eyes. Hubert could tell she was sizing him up. Trying to decide whether to trust him with more information.

"Look, Grandmama, if you want me to retrieve this giant pumpkin of a diamond, you must tell me everything you know!"

"Yes," she said. "I suppose I must."

She went to an ornate silver box displayed on a bookcase.

She gave Hubert another very judgmental look. Satisfied with what she saw, she finally opened the box with the key she wore on a chain around her neck.

"What I am about to show you, Hubert, is a replica. The original was done on parchment and, after many years, deteriorated to dust. It is a treasure map—or so all of Captain Dog Breath's descendants have assumed through the centuries. Unfortunately, none of them proved clever enough to unmask its secrets."

She pulled a small laminated card out of the unlocked silver box and placed it on the side table so Hubert could study it. Sealed in plastic was a sheet of paper illustrated with a collection of hand-drawn shapes. It wasn't parchment, but it was yellowed and faded, like something clipped out of an ancient newspaper.

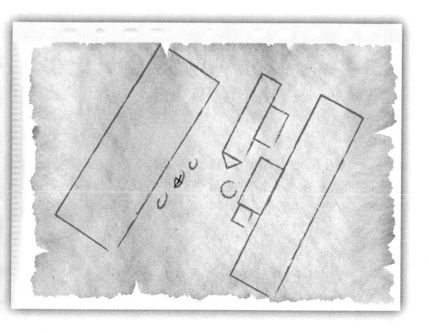

"What is this?" said Hubert. "Some kind of antique cubist art?"

"No, you fool. It is the treasure map your ancestor Aliento de Perro gave to his son, who gave it to his son, and so on until my late husband and then your father came into possession of it." She tapped a tiny X on an oval shape. "That's where the diamond is hidden!"

"Ha!" scoffed Hubert. "This is positively preposterous! A jumble of shapes with no discernible meaning? I'm sorry, Grandmama. I fear our family treasure is lost forever. If only Aliento de Perro had been a better mapmaker!"

Hubert stomped off to his bedroom in a huff.

Fine, thought his grandmother. *If Hubert is too lazy to find my treasure, I will recruit the services of someone else to do it for me.*

She laughed softly as she hatched her scheme.

Someone who will find la Gran Calabaza, thinking, once again, that it is rightfully theirs.

Now her soft laughter grew more intense. Her shoulders shuddered.

Because once the foolish little girl and her brainy chums did all the hard work, Penelope Flippington Huxley would swoop in and snatch the diamond away.

She could be a pirate, too.

She could steal things.

But first she had to help Grace Garcia find la Gran Calabaza.

24

Kojo watched as Jake's fingers flew across the small glass screen of the control panel built into the pedestal of the Red Lion Diamond's display case.

"I upped the encryption," said Jake. "No way will anybody be able to crack this code."

"Unless they're as smart as you, baby," said Kojo. "Too bad the diamond isn't yours, Jake."

"Huh?"

Kojo wiggled his eyebrows. "If it was yours, you could make a ring and give it to Grace!"

"Make a ring out of that gigantic diamond? Grace would have to wear an arm sling whenever she wore it. Plus, she'd immediately know it was the Red Lion and be furious at me for stealing it. Not a very romantic gesture, Kojo."

"Aha! So Grace Garcia *is* your girlfriend!"

"No, she's not."

"Then why are you talking about making romantic gestures?"

"Because you gave me a hypothetical."

"Come on, Jake. Admit it."

"Grace is not my girlfriend!"

And, of course, that's exactly when Grace came running into the lobby with an envelope in her hand.

"Um, did you hear that?" Jake asked.

"Hear what?" said Grace.

"I, uh, burped," said Jake.

"Actually," said Kojo, "it was more of a belch."

Grace waved both her hands like she was trying to disperse all the nonsense wafting in the air around her.

"Secret meeting," she said. "Now!"

She led the way to the janitor's closet.

When the door was closed, Jake whispered, "What's up?"

Grace showed him and Kojo the envelope.

"This!" she said.

"More fan mail?" said Kojo.

"A plea from another charity?" added Jake.

"It's an anonymous tip," said Grace.

Jake studied the envelope. It wasn't postmarked. In fact, there wasn't even a stamp or a return address. Just Grace's name on a label.

"This was hand-delivered to the front office," said Grace.

"Looks like that label came out of a Dymo 450," said Kojo, who knew a lot of random forensic facts like that. "Very common piece of office equipment."

Grace showed Jake and Kojo the typewritten letter.

"Comic Sans font," said Kojo with a quick look to Jake.

Jake nodded. It was the same font that was used in the *I know your secret* note card. Grace was too excited to notice Jake and Kojo exchanging glances and nodding at each other.

"Just listen to what they wrote," she said. She read from the letter.

Dear Miss Garcia:

I have been following the exploits of you and your treasure-hunting friends Jake McQuade and Kobie Sheldrake. . . .

"Come on," muttered Kojo. "Why can't anybody get my name right?"

"That doesn't matter," said Grace, eager to get back to the letter."

"Maybe not to you."

"You're right. It's rude. Names are important. So is pronouncing them correctly."

"Agreed," said Kojo. "Please continue."

Dear Miss Garcia:

I have been following the exploits of you and your treasure-hunting friends Jake McQuade and Kobie Sheldrake. I saw the news report about someone trying to steal the Red Lion Diamond you donated to your school and thought you should know that there was another, even larger diamond on board the pirate ship where your ancestor was a cabin boy. How do I know this? It is not important. I just do. La Gran Calabaza is a mammoth orange diamond worth billions. I have searched for it, lo these many years. Now I am old and retired. I would like to pass on to you the two clues I have followed for many decades to no avail.

1) "Las tres hermanas ostras"
2) The treasure map—a copy of the one hand-drawn by the pirate captain Aliento de Perro

X marks the spot, as they say.
Good luck.

Sincerely,
A Fan

Grace unfolded a second sheet of paper that had been tucked inside the envelope.

It was a map.

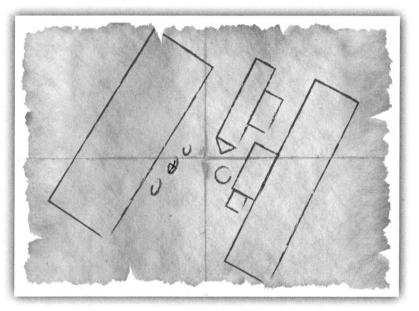

Or a geometry puzzle. Jake wasn't exactly sure.

But he definitely knew what "X marks the spot" meant.

That was where the rest of Grace's pirate booty was buried.

25

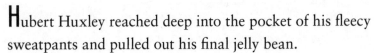

Hubert Huxley reached deep into the pocket of his fleecy sweatpants and pulled out his final jelly bean.

It was pink and covered with lint, but he didn't care.

He wanted to ingest every ounce of knowledge he could.

This one tasted like bubble gum. A bonus.

The effect of the KI jelly beans, the magic capsules similar to those that had made Jake McQuade such a genius, had been almost instantaneous. After the first fistful, Hubert immediately knew all sorts of things he'd never even thought about knowing before.

For instance, the one state in the United States that borders only one other state is Maine. The term *mocha* doesn't come from chocolate but from the port city in Yemen where the drink originated. There are 293 different ways to make change for a dollar. ·

He also knew that his grandmama was up to something.

Something shady.

Hubert had seen her whispering to Chauncy, her chauffeur, early that morning. She had slipped him an envelope, which Chauncy had surreptitiously tucked into his black suit coat. (Hubert now knew that *surreptitiously* meant "in a way that attempts to avoid notice or attention; secretively.")

Chauncy dropped Hubert off at Riverview Middle School that morning. The building was directly across the street from his grandmother's apartment, but arriving in a limousine made a bold statement. When Hubert entered the lobby, Chauncy had pretended to drive away.

But something told Hubert to keep an eye on Chauncy.

After all, Mr. Chauncy Beedle had quite a checkered past. Hubert's father had originally hired Chauncy to do "whatever needs to be done" in his vast real estate empire. If that meant scaring little old ladies into vacating their apartments so Heath Huxley could flip them into "deluxe accommodations" and charge a higher rent, Chauncy was his man.

Chauncy was very good at scaring people.

His grandmother's driver had also kept up his connections with several nefarious members of the criminal underworld. Hubert thought those connections might prove useful as he put his brilliant, jelly bean–fueled master plan into play.

Jake McQuade had been such a fool.

He had ingested Haazim Farooqi's intelligence-expanding magical beans and done what? Helped his friend Grace find some paltry pirate treasure? Won the middle school Quiz Bowl competition and a few basketball games? Wasted time tutoring kids at Riverview?

Ha!

What good was being the smartest kid on earth if you weren't also the richest and most powerful kid, too?

Hubert would do better.

Much, much better!

26

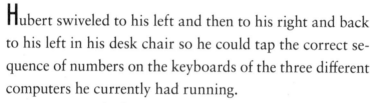

Hubert swiveled to his left and then to his right and back to his left in his desk chair so he could tap the correct sequence of numbers on the keyboards of the three different computers he currently had running.

It was nearly four p.m. Trading would soon end on the New York Stock Exchange as well as the Nasdaq market.

In the hour since he'd been home from school, Hubert had built a mathematical model to anticipate the direction of various investments and engineered his own automated trading system. He'd also gained backdoor access to Mr. Chauncy Beedle's bank account.

He speed-dialed the chauffeur.

"Chauncy?" he said. "Where are you?"

"In the garage with the car."

"Come up to the penthouse. I need you."

"I'm kind of busy, kid" was the reply.

"Too busy to make one million dollars before the markets close?"

There was a slight pause.

"I'm on my way."

Moments later, the driver bounded into Hubert's room. He was panting hard.

"What's this about a million bucks?"

Hubert smirked and spread open his arms to take in all the blinking computer screens.

"You are about to be today's most brilliant day trader, Chauncy. I have devised a foolproof formula to transfer one million dollars into your bank account. Or, if you don't give me the answer I require, that same account will end the day with a zero balance."

"You threatening me, kid?"

Hubert shrugged. "I suppose that depends on what you decide to do."

"What is all this junk?" Chauncy gestured at the green numbers dancing across the three screens.

"Oh, just a little cutting-edge quantitative financial software I threw together. It uses historical data to predict price movements in—"

He stopped. Glanced at the clock in the top right corner of screen two.

"Do you really want all the boring details or that one million dollars?"

"I'll take the million bucks."

"Good. But, before I give it to you, you have to give me something. What was in that envelope Grandmama told you to deliver to the principal's office?"

"You saw me do that?"

"Yes."

"How?"

Hubert gestured to the blinking digits. "The clock is ticking, Chauncy."

"It was for that Grace Garcia girl. The one who beat your old man to the treasure chest. Something about another diamond. 'La Gran Calabaza.' There was a note card with rectangles and circles and ovals and stuff. I couldn't make out many details. There were some other Spanish words in the letter, too. 'Las tres hermanas ostras.' I thought that was weird. Maybe like a secret code or something."

So it was true.

Hubert's beloved grandmama was taking out an insurance policy. His greedy, grasping grandmama had given Grace Garcia the same information she had given him. She wanted the family's treasure-hunting enemies to help her find la Gran Calabaza.

Of course, if Grace, Jake, and Kojo found the jumbo diamond before Hubert, Grandmama would snatch it away from them.

Actually, she'd probably hire Chauncy to do the snatching for her.

Too bad Chauncy wouldn't be available. Because he'd already be on Hubert's payroll.

Hubert hit the enter key.

The transaction went through in a flash.

"Thank you, Chauncy. If you have a banking app on your phone, you might want to check it. See all those zeros we just added to your balance."

"You really made me a million bucks?" Chauncy had his phone out and was eagerly swiping the screen.

"Yes. And I, of course, can do so again. Provided you keep doing things for me."

"You name it, kid, I'll do it. Just like I used to do stuff for your dad."

"Good. Perhaps you could call some of your old chums? The more villainous the better. I think I'm going to need henchpeople. Minions, if you will. All super-villains need minions and henchpeople. I also need a good name. Maybe something piratey, in keeping with my evil ancestor. I know—Captain Brainiac!"

Chauncy gave him a look. "Um, it's a start, Hubert. But, not for nothin', you might want to keep work-shopping your villain name. Maybe something a little more, I don't know, sinister."

"No! You will call me Captain Brainiac!"

"Sure. Fine. Whatever. Just keep adding those zeros to my bank account and I'll call you anything you want, Hubert."

27

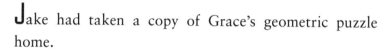

Jake had taken a copy of Grace's geometric puzzle home.

It gave him something to rack his brain over besides the burning questions *Who stole the jelly beans?* and *Which flavor was Zane Zinkle's favorite?*

Because Jake still thought Zinkle was the jelly bean thief.

And Grace's "clue" letter had that Comic Sans font. Just like the card left at the scene of the jelly bean crime.

"Open-and-shut case, baby," said Kojo as they walked to school the next morning. "Zinkle's our man."

"Maybe for the jelly beans," said Jake. "But what about la Gran Calabaza? What's he got to do with that? He already has more money than he'll ever need."

"It's bling. Something bigger and sparklier than anything anybody else has in their vault. You know these tech tycoons. They have trampoline rooms in their basements. They buy James Bond's submarine car. They build rocket ships and go up into space for a minute or two. If there's a three-pound orange diamond out there, Zane Zinkle's gonna want to grab it before one of the other super-rich bad boys does."

Jake nodded, even though he still couldn't figure out the connection between Zane Zinkle and Aliento de Perro or the *Stinky Dog* pirate ship. He'd worry about that later.

Grace would be waiting for them in the janitor's closet. She would assume that, given a solid twelve hours of thinking time, Jake would've cracked the geometry puzzle the way he'd worked the math problem that led to the pirate treasure chest.

The only problem was, Jake was still drawing a blank.

This time he didn't think it was because the jelly beans were wearing off.

"There are no numerical values anywhere on this map," he told Grace and Kojo. They stood around a stack of paper-towel cartons they'd turned into a work desk. The map was on top of it.

"We have five rectangles of various sizes. One square, a circle, and a triangle. Then three ovals."

"Plus the x," said Kojo. "There are a lot of x's in algebra problems."

"But we can't work out any of the dimensions of any of the shapes. And most of the angles are ninety degrees—"

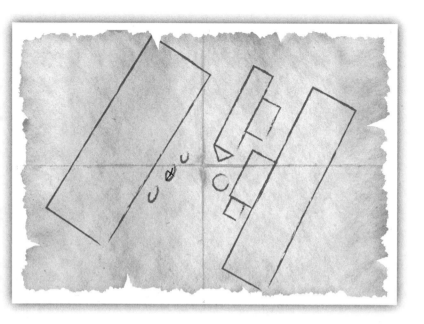

"Except in the circle," said Kojo. "And the ovals? Forget about it. . . ."

"Well," said Jake, "we *could* find angles at given points, say the semimajor axis . . ."

"Wait a second," said Grace. "You're overthinking this, Jake."

"It's what he does best," said Kojo.

"Algebra was the answer last time," said Jake, rubbing his temples, trying to warm up his brain. "This time, the pirates have obviously left us a *geometry* puzzle to figure out."

"Really?" said Grace. "Jake, tell me something: What are the odds that there were *two* genius-level mathematicians aboard the same pirate ship in the late sixteen hundreds?"

"Well," said Jake, "I'd need more data about the

number of math prodigies in the general population before—"

Grace laughed. "¡Tranquilo!" she said.

Which Jake knew was Spanish for "quiet" or, in this instance, "chill."

28

"We know Eduardo Leones was a math whiz," Grace continued. "He left his descendants that complex puzzle as a map to his buried treasure. Do you seriously think the 'foul dragon' who 'snatched the big pumpkin' was some kind of geometry genius? We might be trying too hard with this diagram."

They stared at the puzzle some more.

Jake suddenly had an idea.

" 'Las tres hermanas ostras,' " he mumbled.

Grace nodded. " 'The three oyster sisters.' "

Jake poked a finger at the three small ovals. "Those kind of look like oysters."

"And there's three of them," said Grace. "But how can we tell if they're sisters?"

"Well," said Kojo, "there is a family resemblance. They all look alike. Very ovally."

An even bigger idea started to blossom in Jake's brain. "Hang on. The pirate battle took place right here in New York Harbor, correct?"

"Yep," said Grace. "A British man-o'-war sank the *Stinky Dog*."

"Why did the British call their ship a man-o'-war?" wondered Kojo.

"Kind of sexist, if you ask me," said Grace.

"The 'man-of-war,' or 'man-o'-war,' was the Royal Navy's term for a powerful warship or frigate," said Jake. "They were ships armed with cannons and propelled by sails, not oars."

"Good to know," said Kojo. "Kind of."

"And," said Jake, "speaking of oysters, New York, and the seventeenth century . . ."

"Um, I didn't know we were," said Grace.

"The first people to occupy the three small islands south of Manhattan Island were members of the Lenape tribes, who visited them because of their oyster beds. Eventually, the Dutch, who settled New Amsterdam before the English turned it into New York, referred to the three oyster-rich land masses as the 'three oyster islands.'"

Grace gasped. "¡Las tres hermanas ostras!"

"We need a chart," said Jake.

Kojo nodded. "One of those oyster charts like they have in seafood restaurants?"

"No. A nautical map of New York Harbor from the late sixteen hundreds!"

29

After school, Jake, Kojo, and Grace went to the New-York Historical Society on West Seventy-Seventh Street.

Grace's dad, Professor Garcia, met them there—just in case they needed an adult to gain access to the library's original, antique documents.

Including maps. The museum's library had lots and lots of maps.

"Thanks for doing this with us, Papi," said Grace.

"It's fun," said Professor Garcia. "Doing research in a library is like going on an indoor treasure hunt!"

Grace and her dad led the way up the stone steps, past the bronze statue of Abraham Lincoln, and into the building.

"Psst," Kojo whispered to Jake.

"What?"

"That guy over there. At the hot-dog cart. Don't look. I think he's tailing us."

"How come?"

"He's getting too much mustard on his dog."

"What?"

"It's a classic time waster. He wants to make sure he's not following us too closely."

"So he asks for extra mustard?"

"Exactly. Like I said, it's a classic move."

"You watch too much TV."

"No such thing, baby. If, of course, you've finished your homework and done at least one hour of physical activity, preferably outdoors."

Jake laughed. "Come on."

"Okay. But don't be surprised when the hot-dog dude comes in right behind us."

Jake and Kojo caught up with Grace and Dr. Garcia. Once inside and cleared through security, they all climbed a sweeping staircase to the second floor and the library.

"I registered us online and put in your materials request," Professor Garcia told the group as they entered the reading room, which was pretty impressive—a temple of history with fifty-foot-tall ceilings, stained-glass windows, and marble columns.

"Those are neoclassical columns," said Kojo, who sometimes liked to notice stuff before Jake did. "Love all that Greco-Roman architecture action."

"Please have a seat, Professor Garcia," said the librarian. "I will bring you the map you requested."

"Thank you," Grace's dad said with a smile.

The librarian went off to fetch the document.

"This is what is known as a 'closed stacks library,'" Professor Garcia explained. "The staff will bring everything to us."

"In other words," said Grace, "no browsing, you guys."

"No graphic novels, either," said Kojo, looking around the room disappointedly.

He saw something and kicked Jake under the table.

Because the guy Kojo had spotted at the hot-dog cart had just stepped into the library. He had a bright mustard stain on his shirt and a speck of hot-dog bun trapped in his bushy mustache. He pulled out a notebook and started scribbling in it.

Kojo waggled his eyebrows to say, *See? I told you so.*

Jake didn't think it was all that suspicious.

The guy was just another researcher who'd grabbed a hot dog from a pushcart before coming in to do his scholarly work. Sure, he was a messy eater, but that didn't mean anything.

Or did it?

30

The librarian returned with the antique map.

She was wearing white cotton archivist gloves and treating the ancient paper with the utmost respect. She placed the document on the worktable.

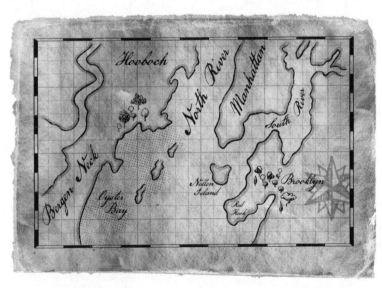

"Per your request, Dr. Garcia, this is New York Harbor from the late sixteen hundreds. You can, of course, see Manhattan and Red Hook in Brooklyn. Over there, close to the shoreline of what we now know as New Jersey, are the oyster banks and their three islands. Only two remain. The third disappeared several centuries later when the railroads added landfill to that shallow area."

"Is it okay to take a picture of this?" Grace asked.

"Yes. There are no copyright issues."

"Cool."

Grace grabbed a shot of the map with her phone.

"Let's head for home."

"That's it?" said Dr. Garcia.

"Yep. This is all we need. Thanks, Papi." She smiled at the librarian. "Thank you, too."

"You're very welcome. And, might I add, it's encouraging to see young people like you engaged in serious research."

"Thanks. My dad's right. It's fun."

"Say, aren't you three the kids who found the buried treasure?"

Professor Garcia gave Grace a proud smile.

"That's right," said Kojo. He put a hand to his mouth to shield what he said next, just in case the hot-dog guy was listening. "And stay tuned. Thanks to you and your map, we might find some more."

31

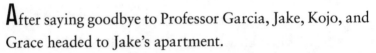

After saying goodbye to Professor Garcia, Jake, Kojo, and Grace headed to Jake's apartment.

Grace texted Jake the map picture she'd snapped in the library. Jake uploaded the photo into a graphics program and carefully lined it up with the image of the geometric-shapes puzzle he'd already scanned into his computer.

"We have a match," he said, working with the app to superimpose the two images. "You were right, Grace. Aliento de Perro wasn't a geometry genius. He was just a horrible cartographer."

"A person who draws maps!" blurted Kojo, like he was giving an answer at the Quiz Bowl.

Grace laughed. "You are correct, sir."

"I guess all Captain Dog Breath could draw were rectangles, triangles, and circles," said Jake.

"And ovals," said Kojo. "Dude could do an awesome oval."

"Check it out," said Jake, filling the screen with his overlay.

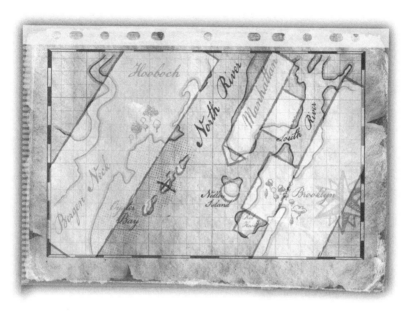

Grace gasped.

"What?" said Kojo. "Why'd you just gasp?"

"Because, those islands. This one here . . ." She touched the northernmost oval. "That's Ellis Island. And this one?" She tapped the oval with the X on it.

"Yep," said Jake. "That's Liberty Island."

"Home of the Statue of Liberty."

"Of course!" said Kojo. "The pirate buried his treasure on Liberty Island because the statue is the perfect landmark. No way could you forget where you buried your pirate booty after you busted out of prison. You'd just have to look for the big green lady holding up a torch."

"Uh, Kojo?" said Grace. "The Statue of Liberty wasn't there in the late sixteen hundreds."

"It wasn't even dedicated until 1886," said Jake, resisting the urge to tell his friends everything he knew about the copper statue. (Like that it was a gift from France, created by the French sculptor Frédéric-Auguste Bartholdi, with interior scaffolding by Gustave Eiffel, the same guy who did the tower in Paris.)

"Uh, yeah," said Kojo. "I know. I was making a joke. This is supposed to be fun, remember?"

"We don't have time for fun," said Jake. "This is important."

Kojo gave him a look. "Jake? You seriously need to lighten up."

"When the *Stinky Dog* sank," said Grace, changing the subject, "Liberty Island was just one of the three oyster islands."

"It's also a fourteen-point-seven-acre land mass," said Jake. "Finding a buried treasure with nothing but an X to work with won't be easy."

"We'll have to dig up the whole island!" said Kojo. "If the Big Pumpkin is really worth all those billions, we can build New York City a new statue when we're done."

"Or . . . ," said Jake.

"Or what?" said Kojo.

"We could call our friends at the Consortium." Jake dug around in his desk to find Dr. Doublé's business card. "They have access to all sorts of surveillance gear. I bet they could find us a satellite equipped with remote sensing technologies. You know—electromagnetic radiation, ground-penetrating radar, sonar. All that high-tech treasure-hunting stuff."

"But," said Grace, "they might want some of the treasure."

Jake gave her a grin. "Why, Grace Garcia. I thought we were doing this for the fun, not the money."

"We are, but . . ."

"I'll have my dad work out the details of their financial involvement," said Kojo. "He's a lawyer. I'm sure the Consortium will do a deal. Don't forget, Jake, you're our biggest bargaining chip. Dr. Doublé wants easy access to you and your ginormous, jelly bean–fueled brain the next time there's some sort of international crisis."

Yeah, thought Jake. *Just as long as I still have that ginormous brain.*

He didn't tell his friends, but Jake hoped Mr. Farooqi would hurry up and finish analyzing the tutti-frutti jelly bean. Figure out what he'd done when he made it and then do it again.

"Wait a second," said Grace. "Liberty Island is a national park. We're going to need a major permission slip before we can go treasure hunting on it."

Jake snapped his fingers. "I'll call Don Struchen."

"Of course," said Kojo, snapping *his* fingers. "Your friend at the FBI!"

"Woo-hoo!" said Grace, snapping her fingers because everybody else seemed to be doing it. "This might work. We're lucky everybody owes you a favor, Jake."

Jake blushed a little.

Grace didn't notice. She was too jazzed. "We should do it early in the morning. That way we won't draw too much media attention."

"Hey," said Kojo, "when we dig up a three-pound diamond worth . . ." He turned to Jake. "How much did you say?"

"Approximately nine billion six hundred and fifty-eight million dollars."

"Yeah. When we find la Gran Calabaza, it's going to be all over the news. Heck, I might even post about it on Insta." Kojo pulled out his phone to record a reminder. "Note to self," he dictated. "Take selfie with Big Pumpkin."

"We need to make some calls, guys," said Jake.

"No," said Kojo. He took Dr. Doublé's business card from Jake. "My dad does."

32

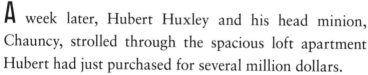

A week later, Hubert Huxley and his head minion, Chauncy, strolled through the spacious loft apartment Hubert had just purchased for several million dollars.

Actually, the shell corporation he'd recently established, with Chauncy as its supposed CEO, had bought the whole building.

"Excellent," said Hubert. "This is the perfect lair."

Chauncy's phone buzzed. He looked at the screen. "It's your grandmother."

"Don't answer it," snapped Hubert. "You work for me now."

"Yes, sir, Captain."

"Captain what?"

"Uh, Brainiac, sir."

Chauncy thumbed his phone and dumped the call.

Skilled movers had delivered and installed the

furniture and high-end toys that Hubert had purchased with credit-card information he had cleverly siphoned off the internet. Well, to any other cyberthief, his methods would seem clever. For Hubert, they were oh so easy.

After all, he was the smartest kid on the planet. Everything came easy to Hubert Huxley, aka Captain Brainiac. Anything he wanted, he could figure out a way to obtain it—for free. And, if money was needed, that was also easy to acquire. His bank account was bulging with cash. So were the bank accounts of the henchpeople Chauncy had recruited.

His spacious supervillain hideout had three eighty-six-inch video screens. The world's most expensive zero-gravity gaming chair. A fully stocked soda-pop vending machine and snack dispenser—no coins needed. His freezer was filled with stacks of gourmet pizzas, prepared by New York's finest pizza chef, whom Hubert now had on speed dial. His cabinets overflowed with Oreos—all eighty-five known flavors, including Cherry Cola, Marshmallow Crispy, and Pumpkin Spice.

Hubert even had a basketball half-court at one end of his sprawling apartment, which used to be some sort of factory floor. Hubert wasn't sure what they used to make. But *he* would make mischief.

He would also make Jake McQuade's life miserable.

His phone buzzed.

"My, my, my," he said. "It's Grandmama. Now she's calling me."

"You gonna answer it?" asked Chauncy.

"I suppose I must."

He thumbed the screen.

"Hello, Grandmama."

"Hubert? Where have you been, you lazy lummox?"

"Setting up my new apartment."

"Your new what?"

"I bought a loft."

"You can't buy an apartment. You're not even a teen-ager!"

"I misspoke. My limited-liability corporation, Captain Brainiac, LLC, made the actual purchase. Only cost twenty-two."

"Twenty-two what?"

"Million, of course."

"How on earth did you get that kind of money?"

"The old-fashioned way. I stole it."

"And where are you going to school? The fools at Riverview Middle called here to inquire about your absence."

"I'm finished with school."

"What?"

"I already know more than anyone else. There is nothing left for me to learn."

"What about going to college?"

"Why bother? I already know more than all the professors who ever taught at all the Ivy League universities combined!"

"Hubert? What's come over you?"

"Let's call it a growth spurt, shall we?"

"You're already a colossus. How could you grow any taller?"

"It is my brain that has become Brobdingnagian."

"What?"

"Brobdingnagian. From Brobdingnag, in Jonathan Swift's *Gulliver's Travels*. That's the name of a land where everything is huge."

There was a pause.

"Hubert? What are you up to?"

"You'll see. This 'lazy lummox' might soon surprise you, Grandmama. Why, I even might make you and Capitán Aliento de Perro proud."

"What do you mean?"

"I am going full pirate. I'm going to find la Gran Calabaza."

"What? How?"

"The same way you intended to. By seeing what Jake McQuade and his friends do with that ridiculous map you gave first to me and then to Grace Garcia."

"You . . . know . . . about . . ."

"I know everything, Grandmama! I am Captain Brainiac!"

He slammed his phone to the floor, shattering it. He kicked at the shards of glass with the toe of his very expensive shoe.

"Chauncy?"

"Yes, uh, Captain Brainiac?"

"I suspect I'm going to need a new phone."

"I'll send Eddie out to fetch you one."

"Fine. But this time, kindly tell him not to stop at any hot-dog carts along the way. All that mustard stuck in his mustache is disgusting!"

33

FBI Deputy Assistant Director Don Struchen called Jake back when all the details had finally been ironed out. "You and your team of . . . extractors . . . will have three hours on the island. This Saturday. From one a.m. until four a.m. The National Park Service has given permission, and I have given *them* certain assurances."

"Thank you, Mr. Struchen."

"No, thank you, Jake. We never would've closed the Karpen file without you."

Once the FBI "signed the permission slip," Dr. Doublé went to work.

All the considerable international resources of the Consortium were put into play. A satellite, outfitted with microwave P-band radar technology developed by scientists in Israel, scanned Liberty Island. It was very good at identifying objects beneath the surface and had been employed in archaeological digs.

"We have identified several possible locations to explore," Dr. Doublé told Jake during an after-school video call.

"Let's just hope the pirate guy buried his treasure in a metal box," Jake replied.

"We suspect he did."

"You've seen it?"

"We think so."

"From your satellite scan?"

"Coupled with some ground-penetrating radar sweeps we did from vessels disguised as tugboats that are currently patrolling New York Harbor."

"This is amazing!" said Jake

Dr. Doublé laughed. "Let's just say with this kind of high-tech gadgetry, finding a needle in a haystack is much easier."

So, that Saturday, at twelve-thirty a.m., Jake, Grace, and Kojo were at the tip of Manhattan Island, ready to board the Consortium's high-speed hovercraft, which would whisk them out to Liberty Island. Jake's mom and Emma were coming along for the ride. Sure, it was way past everybody's bedtime, but it wasn't a school night.

Besides, this was too exciting to miss.

Grace's and Kojo's parents were there, too. So was Principal Lyons.

It was going to be a celebration! Jake, Grace, and Kojo were about to solve a centuries-old mystery and dig up the world's most valuable diamond. That definitely deserved a party.

The hovercraft breezed along above the choppy water, making a beeline for the island. Kojo slid open a window so he could lean into the spray blasting over the bow.

Grace turned to look at her family. They were seated at a table with Uncle Charley and Kojo's and Jake's families. All of them were sipping hot chocolate. They were also devouring brownies, cookies, slices of cake, and assorted hot and cold appetizers. The Consortium had hired a catering company to turn the hovercraft into a party boat.

"Look at our families," she said. "They're all so proud."

"And happy," said Jake, who loved the way his mom was beaming at him.

"Your uncle Charley is probably the happiest," Kojo said to Grace. "Are you going to split your billions with him after we dig up the diamond?"

"Yep," said Grace. "And we want to give you guys like ten percent each of whatever we get for la Gran Calabaza. Call it a finder's fee."

"Um, wouldn't that be like almost a billion dollars?" said Kojo.

Grace winked at him. "Who loves ya, baby?"

"Apparently you," said Jake with a laugh.

The hovercraft docked where the Statue of Liberty tourist boats usually did.

Frankie and three other members of the Consortium's implementation team were the first off the boat. They wore heavy backpacks that reminded Jake of the boxy white ones Apollo astronauts had worn on the moon. Jake figured the backpacks contained high-tech computers of some sort, maybe linked to the handheld metal detecting sensors they were all carrying.

"If you three will kindly follow me," said Dr. Doublé, leading Jake, Kojo, and Grace down the gangplank behind the extraction team.

"Come on, Uncle Charley!" Grace called to Mr. Lyons. He was still in the cabin of the hovercraft, munching on miniature quiches.

"You kids go ahead!" he shouted back.

"Have fun, Jake!" said his mother.

"Oh, I will!"

"¡Eres mi héroe, Jake!" shouted Emma.

That, of course, made Jake feel warm and fuzzy all over. His little sister had just called him her hero!

34

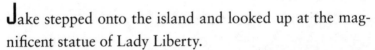

Jake stepped onto the island and looked up at the magnificent statue of Lady Liberty.

Sure, thanks to the jelly beans, he knew all the facts and figures about her. That the broken chains on her pedestal were part of her antislavery, abolitionist symbolism. That she stood as tall as a twenty-two-story building. That Lady Liberty is struck by lightning six hundred times every year. But for now he was just having fun, wondering why she was wearing sandals and who clipped her giant green toenails.

"Fortunately," said Dr. Doublé, "we think the metal treasure chest is right over there in that stand of trees. If it were under the fort at the base of the statue, we would need to undertake major excavation."

Frankie, the Consortium heavy who had driven Jake

to Zinkle headquarters a few weeks earlier, marched with his metal detector into the small thicket of trees.

"I'm getting something, Doc," he called out. "Strong pings. Right where the scans said we might."

"Congratulations, children. As we suspected, the pirate captain secured his giant diamond inside a metal lockbox."

"Can we be the ones to dig it up?" Jake asked eagerly.

"If you wish."

The Consortium leader turned to her crew.

"Lend them your entrenching tools, please."

The heavily equipped Consortium soldiers pulled collapsible, black-bladed shovels out of pouches strapped to their thighs.

"Happy digging," Frankie said to Jake, handing him the tool. Kojo and Grace were given shovels, too.

Frankie scraped an *X* with the toe of his boot in the soggy soil.

" 'X' marks the spot, kids!"

Jake stepped on his blade and scooped out some dirt. Grace went next. Kojo cut into the soil after her. The friends took turns, digging deeper. And deeper.

Soon they were three feet down.

"Nice and easy," coached Kojo. "We're getting closer. We don't want to bust open a rusty old lockbox and scratch the diamond."

"It's a diamond," said Grace. "The hardest substance on earth. It can only be scratched by another diamond."

"Well, maybe these shovels have diamonds on their tips. I can't really tell because—" ,

The tip of Jake's shovel tinked against something.

The three friends immediately dropped to their knees and scraped away the last layer of silt and crumbled rock.

"I see it!" said Grace.

"Me too, baby!" shouted Kojo.

Jake used his shovel to carefully wedge away the clay clamped tight against the sides of the corroded metal box.

When Grace reached down to pull the brittle treasure chest out of its hiding hole, it crumbled in her hands. Flaky pieces and crusty chips fell away.

There was a thud.

Dr. Doublé shone her flashlight down into the hole.

The beam sparkled back in a bedazzling display.

Because it had just hit an oblong, orangish diamond the size of a mini football.

La Gran Calabaza.

35

"Well done, team," said Dr. Doublé. "Well done indeed. We have found the fabled giant pumpkin."

She extracted a long stainless-steel device from her backpack. At its tip was a cluster of prongs. She could open and close them, like the claw at the end of an arcade crane game, by manipulating a plunger at the top.

Dr. Doublé lowered the slender device into the hole and deftly snagged the giant diamond.

"It's heavy," she commented as she carefully pulled la Gran Calabaza up out of its pit.

"Three pounds," said Kojo.

"And we're the first to see it in centuries!" gushed Grace.

"Amazing!" said Jake.

The diamond glistened in the moonlight the instant it cleared the lip of the ditch. Dr. Doublé turned to Frankie.

"François?"

Frankie snapped open a foam-lined carrying case. There was an oval indentation carved into the top and bottom—perfect for safely securing and transporting the priceless artifact.

"Thanks," said Grace. "I didn't think to pack a travel crate for the diamond."

"Of course you didn't," said Dr. Doublé.

Jake wasn't sure, but it looked like she might have a smirk on her face.

"You were too busy thinking about all those billions of dollars you were going to make from its sale, weren't you, Ms. Garcia?"

Frankie clamped the small carrying case shut and stuffed it into his backpack.

"Actually," said Grace, "the majority of the money we raise from the sale of my family's treasure will go, as always, to charitable causes." She held out her hand. "It might be best if *I* transport la Gran Calabaza back to the mainland myself."

"You heard her, Frankie," said Kojo, putting on his best grizzled TV detective voice. "That giant rock belongs to Grace Garcia's family. Fork it over, pal."

Dr. Doublé snickered. So did Frankie. So did the other members of the Consortium crew.

"You children are so amusing," said Dr. Doublé.

"Hysterical," added Frankie.

Jake narrowed his eyes. "What's going on here?"

"Nothing," said Dr. Doublé. "But we'll be invoking that noted legal doctrine I've heard Kojo cite so often: 'finders keeperus, losers weeperus.' The diamond is ours! The Consortium needs it for something much more important than making charitable contributions to questionable causes."

Jake, Kojo, and Grace looked at each other in shock.

Had the Consortium been playing him all along? Jake wondered. Was all that training at their top-secret facility part of some master plan to do . . . something?

Jake knew the Consortium had double-crossed him.

But he had no idea why.

Grace's shock turned to anger. "I'll have you know, Dr. Doublé, that our charitable trust has—"

She didn't get to finish that thought.

Someone dropped out of the sky.

Someone wearing a flight helmet and a backpack with two three-foot-wide enclosed rotors jutting out on either side like circular wings. They were bigger versions of the rotors on a standard quadcopter drone. The pilot used hand controls to tilt and pitch the barrel-sized rotors and ease himself to a soft landing.

"Who's that?" said Kojo. "Iron Man?"

The intruder's boots touched the ground. He flipped up the tinted visor on his helmet.

"Hello, Jake. Hello, Kojo. It's splendid to see you boys again."

It was Zane Zinkle!

36

"**P**er your request, Mr. Zinkle," said Dr. Doublé, "we have, as you see, secured the giant orange diamond."

"Pity you weren't as lucky with the red one at the middle school," said Zinkle. "I really wanted the Red Lion. No, I really *need* it to fulfill my vision!"

"I couldn't crack open the display case or the security system's encryption code," said Frankie.

"Whatever," said Zinkle. "The giant orange diamond is a start."

"A start?" said Kojo. "Just how greedy are you? That puppy's worth billions of dollars!"

Zinkle laughed. "Oh, my poor, misguided young friend. In the proper hands, and coupled with a second large diamond, it is worth much, much more!"

"Yes," said Dr. Doublé. "Our clients are eager for you to complete the device."

"Well," said Zinkle, sounding huffy, "if you and your people had extracted the red diamond as I requested . . ."

"We tried!"

"You failed!"

While Zinkle and Dr. Doublé squabbled, Jake's brain started spinning—like a hard drive grinding as it tries to process an overload of new information.

Frankie was the one who broke into the school and tried to steal the Red Lion?

Okay. That made sense. A former special-forces operative would have the skills to get in and out without leaving any evidence.

But, even with all their high-tech gear, they still couldn't snatch the diamond on display in the school lobby. Jake's shatterproof display case with its supersmart security system had held up. That was good.

The next load of data through his mental processor was harder to compute: The Consortium was working with and/or for Zane Zinkle? They were supposed to be an intergovernmental agency championing good all over the world.

The Consortium had been the ones to reach out to Jake, advising him that their "international clandestine activities" were highly confidential and "under the radar."

"The CIA and FBI don't even know we exist," Dr. Doublé had explained during their first meeting. "But,

Jake, the world needs you. That's why we want to see if you have what it takes to join the Consortium."

Duh. Now it made sense.

Dr. Doublé didn't want Jake talking to his friends in the US intelligence community because the Consortium was only *pretending* to be one of the good guys.

37

"Now then, Jake," said Dr. Doublé, snapping him out of his thoughts. "You and your friends are to return to the hovercraft, enjoy some more delicious party food, and sail home to Manhattan. Forget all about la Gran Calabaza. Forget the ancient treasure map. Forget we ever met. If you report any of this evening's activities to your associates at the FBI or the CIA, I'm afraid your families . . ."

She paused to smile and wave at the hovercraft, docked about a hundred feet away.

Everybody on board smiled and waved back. Jake figured they'd been having so much fun, they hadn't even noticed drone-man Zinkle dropping out of the sky in front of the glowing Statue of Liberty.

Speaking through a tight smile, Dr. Doublé continued. "If you attempt to interfere with our ongoing operations, your families will suffer the consequences of your actions.

We wouldn't want anything to happen at your mother's hotel during her next big event, would we? And your little sister, Emma. Children can be so clumsy. Do I make myself clear?"

"The doctor is giving you sound advice," said Zinkle.

Jake squeezed both hands into tight fists.

He didn't know what to do.

He'd been tricked. The smartest kid in the universe had been acting like a fool.

He'd put his whole family at risk. Kojo's and Grace's families, too.

How would they ever get out of this mess?

Suddenly, several bright floodlights thumped on. They were stationed to the west, behind the statue, over in New Jersey, which was actually closer (less than half a mile) to Liberty Island than New York City was.

"This is Deputy Assistant Director Don Struchen of the FBI," boomed a voice through a megaphone. "We have you and the island surrounded. Place your weapons on the ground. Do it now!"

38

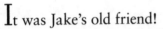

It was Jake's old friend!

Apparently, Mr. Struchen and the FBI hadn't just arranged for Jake and his classmates to go treasure hunting on federal property. They were also keeping tabs on them. Jake's chest untightened. He could breathe again. It was good to have friends—especially ones like Don Struchen.

Outboard engines fired up. Several swift-moving FBI rubber rafts surged across the bay from the Jersey shoreline, heading for Liberty Island.

"Execute extraction package," Frankie barked at his colleagues. "Now!"

Zane Zinkle throttled up his dual rotors and hovered a few feet off the ground.

"You heard the man!" he said. "Deploy your new toys!"

Dr. Doublé and the four Consortium commandos grabbed nylon rip cords dangling from their bulky backpacks and yanked hard.

A pair of drone rotors sprang out on wing struts over the shoulders of each of the five.

The FBI boats bounded over the choppy waters.

They were close and zooming closer.

The human drones revved their whirling rotors and, with a soft whoosh and whirr, lifted off. The giant diamond was snugly stowed inside Frankie's backpack. It'd be leaving Liberty Island with him.

"So long, Jake!" cried Dr. Doublé. "It seems you aren't much of a genius after all!"

"We played you, kid!" added Frankie with a nasty chuckle as he rose into the air. "Like a fiddle!"

By the time the first FBI SWAT team dashed to where Jake, Kojo, and Grace stood beside the empty hole, the six human drones had cleared the well-lit crown of Lady Liberty and angled off to parts unknown.

"You okay, Jake?" It was Special Agent Patrick Andrus. Jake had worked a case with him in the past.

"Yeah. Our families are on that hovercraft."

"Don't worry," said Andrus. "Special Agent Otis has already secured their vessel."

"Roger that," came a voice over Andrus's shoulder-clipped walkie-talkie.

Jake smiled. Kellie Otis. He'd worked a case with her, too.

The families were safe. That was such great news.

But they were soon going to be seriously disappointed.

Because Zane Zinkle and Dr. Doublé had just stolen the giant pumpkin diamond.

The last of the Leones family's treasures.

39

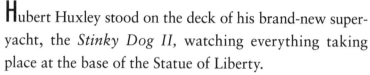

Hubert Huxley stood on the deck of his brand-new super-yacht, the *Stinky Dog II,* watching everything taking place at the base of the Statue of Liberty.

His tracker, Eddie, he of the mustard stains, had tailed Jake McQuade and alerted Hubert to what, as he put it, was "going down."

"Word is they're heading to the Statue of Liberty," Eddie had reported. "Tonight. After midnight. So, technically, I guess they're really doing it tomorrow. In the morning."

Hubert and Chauncy had only had about six hours to prepare.

But when you have access to all the money in the world, you can move fast.

They'd quickly outfitted their new yacht—what Hubert was calling his twenty-first-century pirate ship—with sophisticated long-range viewing scopes and listening devices. They set the equipment up near the wide windows of the party room.

"They're going to dig up my family's long-lost diamond!" Hubert told Chauncy. "Fine. Let them do the sweaty, dirty work. Once they have the diamond, we will board their vessel and steal it away. A treasure stolen by pirates from other pirates and then pilfered by my pirate ancestor from his pirate boss shall, once again, be pirated away."

Chauncy flinched every time Hubert said a word with a *P* in it. Each one came with a popped puff of foul-smelling dog breath.

Thanks to all the high-tech spy gear, Hubert had been able to hear everything being said out on the island.

First Dr. Doublé confirmed that McQuade and company had successfully extracted la Gran Calabaza. They had somehow figured out that ridiculous treasure map.

But, true to her name, Dr. Doublé proceeded to double-cross the gullible dolts from Riverview Middle School. She was going to keep the diamond for herself.

Then things became super interesting.

A mysterious figure descended from the inky sky wearing a double-rotor drone backpack.

He was soon identified as Zane Zinkle, the fabled tech tycoon. He definitely had the brains and skill to engineer the human drone contraption.

Zinkle said something that piqued Hubert's curiosity:

"Pity you weren't as lucky with the red one at the middle school. I really wanted the Red Lion. No, I really *need* it to fulfill my vision!"

Interesting. Zinkle was talking about the diamond on display in the lobby of Riverview Middle School.

Why would Zinkle want it as well as the largest diamond in the world?

Was he, as Kojo Shelton proclaimed, simply greedy? Or was Zinkle plotting to do something with the two enormous diamonds besides sell them?

Dr. Doublé had mentioned something about a "device" and "clients" being eager for its completion.

"What do you want to do, boss?" Chauncy had asked when it was clear that Zinkle was stealing la Gran Calabaza. "Should we storm the island and snatch the stone away from Rocket Man?"

"Let's let it play out," Hubert advised. "I suspect there is more to what is transpiring than we can currently comprehend."

"Fine. Whatever. You're the boss."

"Because," said Hubert dramatically, "I am Captain Brainiac!"

Chauncy cringed a little. "You still going with that name, huh?"

"Yes. Do you have an issue with it?"

"No, boss. I mean, Captain Brainiac. Love the name. Bigly."

Hubert kept watching the action on the island.

Things went sideways fast when, all of a sudden, the FBI showed up.

They stormed the island in rubber rafts.

The diamond thieves deployed drone suits—identical to the one Zinkle had strapped to his back—blasted off, and took to the sky.

That's when Hubert realized what he needed to do.

He dashed down belowdecks to where he'd set up his most sophisticated laptop.

He tapped into a high-resolution radar app.

He locked in on the six flying blips. Soon he would know where they were headed. If Zinkle was up to something even more daring than stealing the largest diamond in the world, that was where it would take place. At his hideout. His lair.

"They're flying north," he announced.

"Good to know," said Chauncy, who'd followed Hubert down into the ship's computer room.

As Hubert watched the blinking blips, he felt like one of those Christmas Eve weathercasters tracking Santa's sleigh on its flight around the world from the North Pole.

But Zinkle and his diamond-thieving companions weren't traveling that far north.

A few hours after liftoff, when Hubert and Chauncy were devouring their second gourmet pizza of the morning (this one was sprinkled with bacon bits, since it was breakfast time), the clump of drones landed in a remote section of New York's Adirondack Mountains. La Gran

Calabaza was now approximately three hundred miles north of Liberty Island.

Hubert's fingers flew across the keyboard, tapping in commands.

He pinpointed the exact location: 625 Hawk Ridge Road, Tupper Lake, New York.

He also had the Google satellite image of Zinkle's remote lakeside lodge. A lovely log mansion.

He knew precisely where to find Zane Zinkle.

More important, he knew where to find his family's long-lost treasure.

40

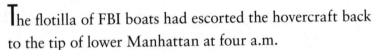

The flotilla of FBI boats had escorted the hovercraft back to the tip of lower Manhattan at four a.m.

The streets were deserted. The city that never sleeps was at least napping. The FBI organized "secure" car rides home for everybody, even though they were confident that "the current threat level is minimal."

"But it still exists," said Kojo. "Am I right?"

"Little bit," said Special Agent Andrus.

"We'll have agents posted outside all your homes," said Deputy Assistant Director Don Struchen. "Zinkle and the Consortium got what they came for. We suspect they will have no further interest in pursuing you children or your families."

When Grace's family and Kojo's were loaded into sleek black sedans and on the move, Struchen turned to address Jake's mother.

"Ms. McQuade?"

"Yes, Deputy Assistant Director Struchen?"

"Please call me Don."

"Phew," said Emma. "That sure makes things easier."

Struchen smiled. "My title barely fits on my business cards." He handed one to each member of Jake's family. "If you need anything, call me."

Jake's mom had a knowing look in her eye. "So, tell me, Don. Why did you hold us back? Why aren't we in a car headed home?"

Struchen grinned. "I see where Jake gets his smarts."

No, you don't, thought Jake, but he didn't dare say it.

"Our being here tonight was not a coincidence," said Struchen. "Once Jake told us he was working with, as he put it, 'the esteemed intergovernmental agency called the Consortium,' all sorts of red flags went up."

"They did?" said Jake.

"Jake, I sure wish you'd called me when the Consortium first reached out to you."

"They said I couldn't tell anybody because everything they did was super secret."

"Because most of it is super illegal. The bureau's been tracking them for years. Those people aren't who they told you they are. They're mercenaries and weapons merchants. Offering their services to the highest bidders."

Jake's mom put a hand over her mouth. Like she might be sick.

"Ha!" laughed Jake's little sister. "And Jake spent like

almost the whole summer with them. He even skipped our trip to Disney World. I thought that was a pretty dumb decision, especially since everybody says Jake is a genius. Hello? It's Disney World."

"I swear I didn't know," said Jake. "I guess I got caught up in all the excitement. It was like I was going to spy school."

"Jake?"

"Yes, Mr. Struchen?"

"Today's Saturday. I was hoping you might be able to spend some time with us later this afternoon. We'd like to learn everything you know about the Consortium."

"Is Jake in trouble?" asked his mom.

"Not with us, ma'am. But there are some seriously bad actors connected with Dr. Doublé and her group. We know she is currently pursuing an illegal arms deal with several hostile nations."

"I can take you to their secret headquarters!" said Jake. "And their training facilities. They have this island with an underground tunnel connecting it to the mainland. I know exactly where it is."

"So do I," said Jake's mom. "We dropped Jake off up there several times."

"It's in a strip mall," added Emma. "There's a frozen yogurt place and a sub shop."

Struchen checked his watch. "The sun's not even up. Why don't you three head home, grab some sleep. Jake? We'll pick you up at fifteen hundred hours."

"That means three p.m.," said Emma.

Jake nodded. "I know, Emma."

"Sorry," she said. "I thought you might be losing all the extra intelligence you picked up this year. After all, you knew absolutamente nada about your summer buddies."

Emma was right. Jake hadn't been very smart in his dealings with the Consortium.

He hadn't been very smart at all.

"Let's make it fourteen hundred hours, sir," said Jake. "Two o'clock. We need to bust these guys ASAP!"

41

"You sure we can't come with you?" asked Kojo.

He and Grace were on the sidewalk with Jake, who was waiting for the FBI to pick him up and drive him back to Sunny Smiles Dental.

"No," said Jake. "This could be dangerous."

"So why are *you* going?" asked Grace.

"Because this is all my fault. I lost your family's biggest treasure because I let Dr. Marie Doublé flatter me. 'The world needs you, Jake. The world needs your big, beautiful brain.'"

"Question," said Kojo. "How can any brain be beautiful? I mean, I've seen illustrations. And Mr. Bednarski has that plastic model sitting on his desk in science class. The brain looks gnarly. Like a mound of squiggly gray turkey gizzards or slimy sausages all stuffed inside a hard candy skull . . ."

"Gross, Kojo," said Grace.

"Exactly. That's what I'm saying."

"Anyway, I think Jake's brain is pretty cool," said Grace. "Especially when he's doing good with it."

Jake blushed. That happened a lot around Grace.

"Um, thanks," he said. "I promise I won't do anything dangerous."

A convoy of six SUVs screeched to a halt at the curb. The bulky vehicles were black with smoky tinted windows. A door swung open.

"Hop in!" said someone inside.

Jake leaned in.

It was Special Agent Andrus.

"Oh, hi, Patrick. I was just—"

"In!" barked Andrus. "We need to be OTM."

"That means 'on the move,'" said Kojo.

Jake turned around. "I know what 'OTM' means, Kojo."

"Well, I just wanted to—"

"In!" Andrus shouted. "Now!"

"See ya," Jake said to his friends.

He gave them a nervous wave.

Grace looked worried. Wow. Maybe she had feelings for Jake, too.

Agent Andrus grabbed Jake by the back of his shirt and yanked him into the SUV.

The vehicle lurched away from the curb, tires squealing.

Andrus jammed Jake's seat belt into its buckle for him.

"Thanks." Jake grabbed hold of the overhead door handle. The SUV was moving fast.

"We fed the address you gave us to the GPS," said Andrus.

Blue lights strobed.

Sirens whooped.

The FBI convoy barreled up the avenue, scaring any and all civilian vehicles out of its way.

It was awesome! Like riding in a presidential motorcade. Not that Jake had ever actually done that. But this had to be what that felt like. They owned the road.

"We'll lose the sirens and lights when we're two miles out from the target," Andrus explained. "Don't want to scare away the fish."

Jake assumed the "fish" were Dr. Doublé and her associates. Including Frankie. Jake had liked Frankie, and Frankie had seemed to like Jake, too.

But it had all been a charade. They were double agents. Using Jake—for what? His time with the Consortium had been all about tests. They'd never really asked him to *do* anything. So what had been the purpose of his undercover summer school?

"Do you think Dr. Doublé will still be there?" Jake asked Andrus as, nearly an hour later, the caravan cruised past the Hilton Garden Inn where Jake had, basically, spent his whole vacation so he could be on call for the Consortium. At least the Hilton had a free breakfast buffet with Froot Loops.

"Even if she isn't," said Andrus, "we're hoping to find evidence of where she might be."

"Approaching the target," said the driver.

"We're ready to rock and roll," said the agent up front.

The caravan swooped into the parking lot of the strip mall.

Doors flew open.

FBI agents in SWAT gear stormed out of all the vehicles and, crouching low, dashed toward the dentist's office. A few customers at the sub shop next door lost meatballs from their sandwiches, gawking at the onslaught.

Two agents in flak jackets reached the door first. Another pair with a battering ram stood at the ready behind them.

"Go!" commanded Andrus. "Breach the door. Go, go, go!"

The lead agents tried the door.

It swung open easily.

The sound of mellow easy-listening music wafted on the breeze.

Jake smelled mouthwash.

Over a dozen agents in full body armor trundled into the lobby.

The receptionist looked up from her desk with a toothy smile.

"Hello," she said calmly, glancing at the calendar on her computer screen. "Do any of you folks have an appointment?"

42

"The dentist's office is just a dentist's office again," said Deputy Assistant Director Don Struchen.

Jake had gone with special agent Andrus to a nearby FBI field office for a debriefing.

"Apparently, Dr. Jared Shore closed down his practice over the summer for remodeling. He had no idea that his offices were being used by notorious international mercenaries and arms merchants."

"But what about the elevator in the supply closet?" Jake insisted.

Andrus shook his head. "Gone. Nothing in there except free samples of dental floss and toothbrushes, plus a few pamphlets on why we should all buy a Waterpik to fight gingivitis."

Struchen nodded. "Sound advice."

Jake couldn't believe what he was hearing.

"What about the island? They had this cinder-block building filled with booby traps and mind games for me and Kojo to play."

"The island is now deserted. However, we did notice heavy-equipment tire treads in a muddy spot."

"They bulldozed it all?" said Jake. "They closed up that tunnel back to the shore?"

"So it would seem."

"Wait a second. You guys believe me, right?"

"Of course we do."

"Kojo was there with me for some of the time. He'll back me up."

Struchen sat on the edge of a desk. "Take it easy, Jake. We believe you. But we also know that the Consortium is extremely well financed. They could build all that, make you believe their big lie, and then dismantle it all in a flash."

"Of course," said Jake, remembering an old TV show he'd watched with Kojo. "Just like on *Mission: Impossible*. They were always building elaborate sets to trick people into doing stuff. But Dr. Doublé never asked me to *do* anything. It was all just puzzles and brain games."

Struchen nodded grimly. "Because, Jake, we suspect she only wanted you as bait."

"Bait?"

"To lure Zane Zinkle out of hiding."

"Why? Did they need help with their computers?"

162

"Before you exposed his diabolical brain-drain scheme, Zinkle Inc. made more than half of its profits designing advanced weapon systems."

"The gang down at Langley," said Andrus, referring to the CIA, "suspects that right before you busted him on his AI shenanigans, Zinkle was close to developing a superweapon of some sort."

"They further suspect," said Struchen, "that Dr. Doublé heard about his plans and wanted first dibs on the device for a client eager to go to war with its neighbors. And, of course, Zane Zinkle wanted first dibs on you, Jake."

Jake nodded. "Darth Vader always comes back to wreak his revenge."

"Until, with Luke's help, he turns away from the dark side of the Force," said Andrus.

"True," said Struchen. "But we don't think Zane Zinkle will ever use the Force for good."

"Wait a second," said Jake. "If Zinkle was after me, why didn't he just grab me on Liberty Island?"

"We think," said Struchen, "the big orange diamond might be even more important to Zinkle than you."

"So what do we do next?" Jake asked.

"You go back to school on Monday," said Struchen. "We'll try to find where Zinkle, Dr. Doublé, and her team flew with those drone packs."

"Those things were awesome," said Andrus.

Struchen gave him a grim look. "If we had known

they were going to pull that aerial disappearing stunt, we would've brought along some high-resolution radar gear to track them. Now, as I said last night, Jake, you will notice several agents near your school and apartment building this week. Grace's and Kojo's homes, too. We don't have any actionable intelligence, but well . . . better safe than sorry."

Jake's phone started blaring the brassy theme song from *Kojak*. It was Kojo's ringtone.

"Hey, Kojo," said Jake. "Don't worry. The FBI has our backs."

"And," said Kojo, "somebody else has our diamond."

"I know," said Jake. "I was there, remember? There was a big statue of a lady holding a torch. . . ."

"Not that diamond," said Kojo. "The cops are crawling all over the school. Somebody stole the Red Lion!"

43

"Excuse me, Hubert?" said Chauncy.

Hubert didn't respond.

So Chauncy rolled his eyes and said, "Captain Brain-iac?"

"This had better be important," Hubert finally replied.

"It's your grandmother. She's down on the sidewalk. She insists that we let her in."

"Did she bring freshly baked chocolate chip cookies?"

Chauncy went to the loft's wide windows and looked down to where his old boss, Penelope Flippington Huxley, was using her purse to thwack one of the burly body-guards stationed at the front door.

"Nope," he told Hubert.

"Then send her away. If she will not leave voluntarily, kindly ask Amir to escort her home. I am too busy to deal with her this weekend."

Hubert held up the massive red diamond known in certain circles as the Red Lion. It shimmered under the illuminated magnifying lens he was using to examine it more closely.

"And, once you have dealt with Grandmama, please hurry back. I need to visit a certain professor at Warwick College."

"Um, don't want to, you know, question your plans there, Captain, but it *is* the weekend. The college is probably closed."

"Trust me, Chauncy. Professor Garcia will want to see me."

"All righty, then. Let me send Granny packing, and then you and me are goin' to college!"

"You and I."

"I know. We'll go together." Chauncy scurried out of the loft.

Grandmama, of course, didn't know how busy her "lazy" grandson had become. As Captain Brainiac, he had things to do. Schemes to plot. Mysteries to solve.

For instance: Why did Zane Zinkle need two enormous diamonds?

Hubert had a hunch. Actually, it was more than a hunch. It was an extremely well-educated guess.

He would soon confront Zinkle and all those working with him—Dr. Doublé and the crew that had double-crossed McQuade on Liberty Island. Because if the tech mogul was doing what Hubert suspected he was, then Captain Brainiac wanted to be the one doing it instead.

Hubert rotated the intensely colored red rock. Fiery light sparkled off the diamond's many facets.

The security system that McQuade had set up for the red gemstone's display case had been challenging. Hubert doubted if any jewel thief on earth could have opened it. But Hubert Huxley wasn't a common jewel thief. He was a supervillain. He was Captain Brainiac!

And his was a mind to be feared.

A mind that could crack any code ever concocted.

But before challenging the former child prodigy Zane Zinkle, Hubert thought it wise to intimidate him first.

To let him know exactly who he was dealing with.

The *new* smartest kid in the universe!

44

Hubert needed to buy a little time.

The major markets were closed until Monday morning. Some monetary manipulation would be called for. Some more bank-account meddling.

So this weekend would be spent in a media blitz.

"Fido?" he said to the computer screen on his right. "Call Professor Gimoaldo Garcia."

"Calling Professor Garcia," said Fido, the digital assistant that Hubert had created because Siri and Alexa kept mangling everything he mumbled. Fido, named in honor of the *Stinky Dog,* had only taken an hour to design, code, and install. Because, yes, thanks to the jelly beans, Hubert Huxley was that good of a software engineer.

"This is Dr. Gimoaldo Garcia," said a recorded voice. "I am away from my office. Please leave a message."

Hubert waited for the beep.

And then he made his demands known.

"Professor Garcia, this is Hubert Huxley. Not too long ago, you and your panel of so-called experts ran a battery of intelligence tests on twelve-year-old Jake McQuade. Immediately afterward, you held a press conference and proclaimed, 'He is, without a doubt, the smartest kid in the universe.' Well, Dr. Garcia, that proclamation was inaccurate. For you failed to administer those same, or similar, tests to me. I insist that you immediately rectify this situation. Give *me* the tests you gave McQuade. Then give me something even more difficult. I am available all day today and tomorrow. For the record, I am twelve years old, just like McQuade. But I guarantee you, Professor, I will score much higher than he did. For I, sir, am Captain Brainiac!"

He ended the call.

To be certain that he would not be ignored, Hubert had his digital assistant send the same message via text, email, and voice to all the learned professor's addresses and contact numbers—some public, some theoretically private. How Hubert came to know that information was his secret.

While Fido robotically bombarded the professor with requests, it was time for Hubert's next hack.

He had to break into a television network's main-frame computer and contact the contestants currently

169

scheduled to appear Monday night on *Quiz Zone,* which was broadcast live. Those appearances would be rescheduled for a later date.

Because *Quiz Zone* was also part of the diabolical supervillain Captain Brainiac's master plan.

45

"It's him," Jake whispered to Grace and Kojo. "That's why he demanded these IQ tests. I was wrong about Zane Zinkle. Hubert Huxley is the one who stole Mr. Farooqi's jelly beans!"

Jake, Kojo, and Grace were seated in the top row of an empty lecture hall at Warwick College. It was the same amphitheater where Dr. Garcia and his associates had tested Jake. The three friends were, more or less, hidden in the shadows. Hubert Huxley wouldn't be able to see them watching.

It was Sunday afternoon. Professor Garcia (after numerous robocalls, texts, tweets, and emails from Huxley) had agreed to reconvene his IQ testing panel to see if what Hubert claimed was true.

"You're probably right," said Kojo. "Must be why he

stopped coming to school. He already knows everything there is to know."

"That's impossible," said Grace. "There are always new discoveries to be made and new things to learn. That's what makes life exciting."

"Hey, Jake," said Kojo, "how come *you* keep going to classes?"

"Hmm?" said Jake. He was distracted.

"Why do you go to school? You don't need to be there. You're just like Hubert."

"No, he is not," insisted Grace.

"I meant intellectually," said Kojo. "Not, you know, personality-wise."

Jake nodded. Not because he agreed with Kojo but because he'd just figured out something else.

"The jelly bean thief is also the jewel thief," he whispered. "Hubert Huxley stole the Red Lion!"

"How can you be sure?" asked Grace.

"Because," said Kojo, catching on, "Jake designed a security system that only someone as smart as or smarter than him could crack. Am I right?"

"Yep," said Jake.

"That means Zinkle is off the suspect list. We know he's not as super intelligent as Jake. Heck, I outsmarted Zinkle, too!"

"But," said Jake, "if Hubert ate all the jelly beans he stole from Farooqi, we are, most likely, intellectual equals.

He could've deciphered what I did with the security system and countered it. Of course, there's no way for us to *prove* that Hubert is our diamond thief."

"Yeah," said Kojo. "Because, once again, he didn't leave any evidence. He even knew how to short-circuit all the school's security cameras before he made his entrance."

"Because he knows as much about everything as Jake does," said Grace. "And we can't tell the FBI what we know without revealing the truth about the jelly beans and ruining Mr. Farooqi's life."

"Hey, Jake," said Kojo. "You ever think about taking up a life of crime? You'd be good at it. You could be a criminal mastermind."

"Shhh," whispered Grace. "Here they come."

Professor Garcia and his three colleagues from the Education and Psychology Departments sat in the front row of the auditorium. Hubert sat at a small desk. There was a pitcher of water and a glass, but no pencil, no paper, no calculator.

"I was ready to do this yesterday," Hubert complained.

"We, unfortunately, were not," Dr. Garcia replied politely. "Shall we proceed?"

"Bring it on, old man."

"Oh-kay," Grace grumbled through gritted teeth. "He may be super intelligent, but he's also super rude."

"Super-bad breath, too," added Kojo. "He should've eaten more of the mint-flavored jelly beans."

Dr. Garcia delivered the first question off a card at the top of a very tall stack. "*Book* is to *reading* as *fork* is to (a) *drawing,* (b) *writing,* (c) *stirring,* or (d) *eating.*"

"Really?" said Hubert. "Must we start with the kindergarten-level questions?"

"What is your answer, Mr. Huxley?"

"*D*, of course. *D* for *duh*! *Eating.* Next question. And, please—skip ahead. Jump to the genius-level material!"

"Very well," said one of the other professors, pulling a card from the center of the stack. "In 1990, a person is fifteen years old. In 1995, that same person is ten years old. How can this be?"

Hubert snorted a backward laugh. "Easy. They were born in 2005. *BC!* Therefore, you count backward. Next question."

The third professor projected a slide on a video monitor.

YELLOW = YELLOW
RED = ORANGE
BLUE = ?

"If yellow equals yellow," she said, "and red equals orange, what does blue equal? Black, pink, green, or purple?"

"Depends," said Hubert.

"I beg your pardon?"

"You have two possible answers, lady. Depending on what pattern you are attempting to discern. Yellow plus red, obviously, equals orange. But, for blue, do we mix blue and the color just above it, as we did with red and yellow to make orange? If so, the answer is purple. Or do we keep yellow as our constant, mix it with blue, and wind up with green?"

The professor turned to Dr. Garcia. "The answer I have is green."

"Which, unfortunately, is wrong," said Dr. Garcia. "Hubert is correct."

"Oh, yay," said Hubert sarcastically. "Do I get bonus points every time I point out your mistakes?"

"Moving on," said the fourth professor. "Tabitha likes cookies but not cake. She likes mutton but not lamb. She likes okra but not squash."

"Picky eater," commented Kojo.

"Following these same rules," the professor continued, "would Tabitha like cherries or pears?"

"Cherries," said Hubert. "For whatever strange reason, Tabitha only likes food with two syllables. Come on, Professors. Try harder. Please use your brains so I can use mine!"

46

The testing went on for three full hours.

Grace and Kojo got fidgety. Then they got bored.

Jake, on the other hand, was on the edge of his seat.

Hubert was brilliant. Super brilliant.

There were more math puzzles.

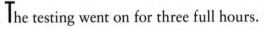

$$11 \times 11 = 4$$
$$22 \times 22 = 16$$
$$33 \times 33 = ?$$

"The answer is thirty-six," said Hubert.

Jake nodded. Hubert was right. Again. Because one plus one times one plus one equals four. Two plus two times two plus two equals sixteen. Therefore, three plus three times three plus three equals thirty-six.

When the professors had exhausted their towering stack of official questions, Professor Garcia gave Hubert a classic riddle. The same one, once upon a time after a basketball game, he had given to Jake.

The same one Jake couldn't figure out in the thirty seconds Dr. Garcia had given him to answer.

"This riddle first appeared in a 1730 manuscript," Dr. Garcia said to Hubert. He wasn't holding any note cards. He had this riddle memorized. "You will have thirty seconds to solve it."

"Did McQuade give you the correct answer?" Hubert asked with a smirk.

"No, Mr. Huxley. He did not."

When they heard that, Kojo and Grace weren't bored anymore. They were on the edges of their seats, too.

"Excellent," said Hubert, rubbing his hands together. "Riddle away, Dr. Garcia."

" 'As I was going to St. Ives, I met a man with seven wives. Each wife had seven sacks. Each sack had seven cats. Each cat had seven kits. Kits, cats, sacks, and wives. How many were there going to St. Ives?' "

Hubert grinned. "McQuade couldn't figure that out?"

"You have twenty seconds," said Dr. Garcia.

"What a dunderhead. And you hailed him as the smartest kid in the universe?"

"This question wasn't on his IQ test."

"It should've been!"

"Ten seconds."

"One!" shouted Hubert. "The answer to your ridiculous riddle is *one*. If the narrator of your little ditty is going *to* St. Ives, then the motley crew with all their assorted cats and sacks and kittens are coming *from* St. Ives. Therefore, there is only one going to St. Ives. Just like there is only one smartest kid in the universe. Me!"

Later, at a packed Sunday evening press conference, the professors from Warwick College proclaimed Hubert Huxley to be the new smartest kid in the universe. Jake, Grace, and Kojo were in the audience, behind a mob of TV camera crews.

"He's smarter than Jake McQuade?" asked a reporter.

"Yes," Professor Garcia admitted.

Jake wished he could disappear into the floor. He didn't have to. No one knew or cared who he was. They were too focused on the next big thing: Hubert Huxley.

"You people may call me Captain Brainiac!" said Hubert.

The press people snickered. Hubert glared. He didn't like snickering.

"Cease your laughter, you simpering fools," he boomed. "Did you not hear the professor? There is no one on earth more intelligent than I! For I know everything!"

A reporter near the front shook her head. "That's what they told us about Jake McQuade."

"Well," sneered Hubert, "they were wrong."

"Isn't your father the billionaire real estate developer Heath Huxley? Wasn't your dad the one who tried to kill Jake McQuade and his two friends?"

"I don't recall," said Hubert.

"He wanted to bulldoze Riverview Middle School and put up a condominium tower."

"I don't recall."

"What about your cousin?" barked another reporter. "Patricia Malvolio. Wasn't she part of that plot, too?"

"I don't recall."

The cluster of reporters laughed.

"You don't recall?" scoffed one. "You just told us you know everything."

"I know everything worth knowing, you chuckle-headed clowns," Hubert said, seething. His face turned pink. His eyes narrowed into slits. "And to prove it, I hereby challenge the former 'smartest kid in the universe,' Jake McQuade, to a one-on-one competition. Tomorrow night. Seven p.m. Live! I think the producers of *Quiz Zone* will be more than happy to have us!"

47

"**C**hallenge accepted!" shouted Kojo from the back of the room.

The TV cameras whipped around. A bevy of bright halogen lamps blinded Jake, Kojo, and Grace.

"That's right," said Kojo, who loved the spotlight. "You heard me, baby. I'm Kojo Shelton, Jake McQuade's manager. And he'll be there for the Battle of the Brains, Monday night at seven, six central. Hubert Huxley is going down. Jake's gonna float like a butterfly and sting like a PhD!"

And that's how Jake, Grace, and Kojo ended up back in the *Quiz Zone* dressing room on Monday night.

"We're so happy you're available," the show's producer

had told Jake earlier in the day. "There was some kind of computer glitch. The contestants who were originally scheduled for tonight received messages to stay home! Weird, huh?"

Jake had appeared on the hit game show once before. He'd defeated two all-time champions in a show billed as the smartest kid in the world versus the world's smartest adults.

Now it would be McQuade versus Huxley for the title of smartest kid in the universe.

"I wonder what the Martian kids think about that," joked Grace.

Jake didn't laugh. In fact, he hadn't chuckled once since he'd figured out that Hubert Huxley was the jelly bean thief. That he was as artificially intelligent as Jake was.

Or was Hubert even smarter?

Because he started out smarter?

Jake was feeling sick to his stomach.

This live TV game show could be a major embarrassment.

No.

It could be a total disaster. A dumpster fire. What they called a "dog's breakfast" over in England, which Jake only knew they said in England because of Haazim Farooqi's jelly beans.

Jake wondered if he should go to the FBI. Convince them that Hubert Huxley was the one who stole the Red

Lion Diamond. If they rushed in and arrested Hubert, then he couldn't do the *Quiz Zone* show.

But there still wasn't any proof. If Jake ran to the feds, they'd probably think he was just trying to avoid dueling with Hubert on national TV.

Plus, Jake couldn't tell anybody about Hubert's other crime—stealing the jelly beans from Farooqi. That would mean admitting that Jake was a jelly bean–fueled fraud, too. It would expose Farooqi before the real genius in this story was ready to go public with his incredible creation.

Jake's hands were tied.

There was no backing out of this.

"Yoo-hoo," said Grace, popping her fingers near Jake's ears to snap him out of his trance. "Earth to Jake. Are you in there?"

"Yeah," he said.

"Come on, baby," said Kojo, "loosen up. You've got this thing."

"Hey, remember that April Fools' Day in the cafeteria?" said Grace. "They had that lemon cake with yellow frosting. You scraped the frosting off, squirted on some mustard, swirled it around, made the mustard look like frosting, and gave it to me? I almost lost my lunch!"

Jake nodded sheepishly. "I'm sorry. That was very immature of me."

"No, dude," said Kojo. "It was very funny. Just like the sponge cake you fooled me with. The one made with a sponge. Besides, it was April Fools' Day, so you had a legit reason to punk Grace."

Grace laughed. "I was a little mad at first. But I had to admit it was funny."

"We should pull something like that on Hubert!" said Kojo. "Knock him off his game. Maybe a water balloon filled with cherry Kool-Aid. We could rig it with a string and a safety pin and . . ."

Jake shook his head.

"Come on," pleaded Kojo. "Goofing around and having fun was your original superpower."

"Sorry. But tonight I need to focus on my new one. Being a genius."

48

When *Quiz Zone* went on the air, Haazim Farooqi was in his lab, running the final tests on the speckled tutti-frutti jelly bean.

For almost a month, he'd scanned, sampled, extracted, extruded, flame-tested, electrochemically analyzed, spectroscoped, and electron-microscoped his one remaining bean. It was definitely the worse for all the wear and tear.

"So much data." He pushed up his safety goggles and wiped his brow with a wad of paper towels clamped in a pair of forceps. "But we should have our answer soon, my teeny-weeny beanie-weenie friend."

Farooqi's computer started crunching the numbers and churning the data. It would need a half hour to finish, which was perfect, because *Quiz Zone* was a thirty-minute show. Farooqi clicked on his tiny lab television, popped open a bag of Chillz Chatpata potato sticks, and settled in to watch Subject One go up against Hubert Huxley.

According to Jake's telling of the sad and harrowing tale, Hubert was the one who had broken into Farooqi's apartment. He was the one who had stolen and devoured the most recent batch of jelly beans.

On the TV, the host introduced the contestants.

In a way, Haazim Farooqi could not lose. Both horses in this race had his jelly beans in their feed bags. But Farooqi was rooting for Jake. He was, and always would be, Subject One. Jake had also become a friend. And, as the old saying went, "The friend appears in hard times, not only at big dinners."

Hubert? At best he was Subject Two. At worst he was nothing but a common, ordinary jelly bean thief, hoping to enjoy a big dinner of fame and glory at Jake's expense.

For the entire game, Jake and Hubert remained neck and neck, each one deftly answering the quizmaster's questions. The questions and answers pinged and ponged like, well, a game of Ping-Pong. Jake answered every question that came his way, but he seemed nervous.

"What is the world's deepest lake?"

"Lake Baikal in Russia."

"When was the first New Year's Eve ball drop in Times Square?"

"December 31, 1907."

"Which is the only US state whose name ends with three consecutive vowels?"

"Hawaii!"

The score remained tied, through many commercials, all the way to the end.

The final question was always the hardest. The contestants would have thirty seconds to write down their answers.

"All right, Jake and Hubert," said the host.

"I told you!" fumed Hubert. "Call me Captain Brainiac!"

"Answer this next question correctly and I just might. For the whole game, what are the names of Earth's five oceans? You have thirty seconds to write down your answers."

Tick-tock music started.

Hubert immediately started writing down his answer. Jake did not. Hubert was scribbling away. Jake was not.

Why?

Surely Subject One knew the answer.

"Atlantic, Pacific, Arctic, Indian, and Southern," Farooqi said directly to the television screen, hoping Jake could somehow hear him on the other side of the glass.

Hubert put down his pen. He had a smug look on his face.

Finally Jake wrote something on his answer screen.

The clock music ended and a buzzer sounded.

"All right, contestants," said the host. "This is it. But, before we reveal your answers, let me just say what a pleasure it's been having these two brilliant young minds on

Quiz Zone. And to think—both of you attend the same public school, Riverview Middle."

"That school is dreadful," said Hubert. "I quit going because they couldn't teach me anything I didn't already know. Don't forget, I'm—"

"Captain Brainiac," said the host with an eye roll. "Okay, Jake. You're our returning champion. What did you write down as the names of the five oceans?"

Jake's answer was revealed: *Atlantic, Pacific, Indian, Arctic, Antarctic.*

"Oh, I'm sorry," said the host. "That is incorrect."

Farooqi hung his head in disbelief. "Oh dear. I should have yelled the answer more loudly at the TV screen." He cupped his hands to make a megaphone. "My bad, Subject One. Please forgive me."

The host turned to Hubert. "Let's see what our challenger wrote down as his answer."

Hubert's answer was revealed: *Arctic, Atlantic, Indian, Pacific, Southern.*

"That is correct!" said the host.

"I know," said Farooqi just as Hubert Huxley said it, too.

"I know. I also listed them in alphabetical order."

"We would've taken any order, Hubert."

"Captain Brainiac!"

The host chuckled. "Well, you are the new champion and the new smartest kid in the universe, so I guess I should call you Captain Brainiac."

"Yes. You should." Hubert glared into the nearest camera. "You all should! Knowledge is power, as you shall soon see!"

"Oh-kay," said the host, turning to Jake. "Jake, thanks for playing. You'll be going home today with a lovely consolation prize. Johnny? Tell him all about it."

"Congratulations, Jake McQuade! This Broyhill recliner—"

Farooqi clicked off the TV set.

He couldn't believe what he'd just seen.

Subject One had lost.

Subject Two had won.

"I must've made the jelly beans stronger this time!" Farooqi gasped. "I put in something different. I changed the recipe. I accidentally made Hubert Huxley smarter than Jake McQuade. Sometimes I do not recognize my own brilliance!"

There was a soft chiming from his computer.

The final test results were in.

Farooqi scanned the screen.

And realized he wasn't as smart as, only seconds ago, he'd assumed he was.

He needed to call Subject One.

This was a bad news/good news situation.

And the bad news? It was very, very bad.

49

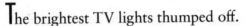

The brightest TV lights thumped off.

Jake and Hubert were standing side by side at their podiums in the studio.

"I know your secret," Hubert whispered.

The same words that had been on the card at Farooqi's apartment!

Hubert Huxley was confessing. He *was* the jelly bean thief.

"I know your secret because now we share it. But my intelligence was already highly advanced before I ingested Haazim Farooqi's creative confectionary concoctions. By the way, that was an example of alliteration."

Jake was too stunned to speak.

"Chauncy?" cried Hubert.

A thick-necked man stepped out of the darkness.

"Yeah, Cap'n?"

"We need to move on to phase two of my master plan."

"You got it, kid. Let's rock and roll."

"Out of my way, peons!" Hubert hissed at the audience members blocking his path. "Stand aside, you scurvy scallywags!"

They moved. Mostly because his hissing was extremely stinky.

Jake's mother came up to him at the podium he was still gripping with both hands. She and Emma had been in the audience, of course, watching the show. "I'm glad you never let being super smart go to your head like *that* young man."

"Yeah," mumbled Jake. He was paler than usual. Because he was terrified. That question about the oceans? The answer had been lost in the fog of another dead zone.

"So you missed one question," said Grace as she and Kojo made their way to the stage.

"Sure, it was the last one," said Kojo. "The most important one in the whole game. But that's okay. You're still you. We still love you, baby."

"We all do," added Jake's mom.

"You're okay, I guess," said Emma.

Suddenly, Jake's phone started playing its *Twilight Zone* ringtone. It was Haazim Farooqi.

"Um, excuse me, guys. I think I need to take this. It's my, uh, quiz coach."

Emma turned to her mother. "Jake has a quiz coach?"

Her mother shrugged. "I haven't been able to keep up with what's going on with Jake for months now."

Jake stepped off into the wings and found a semi-private spot behind the scoreboard.

"Mr. Farooqi?"

"Greetings, Subject One. So sorry about the game show's outcome. I saw you go down in ignominious defeat on live national television. Subject Two laid a beating upon you, as they say. That has to sting."

"Yeah."

"Well, I have good news."

"You finally finished your research?"

"Correct! And Hubert Huxley won't be the smartest kid on the planet for long."

"What do you mean?"

"You were right, Subject One. The beneficial effects of my Ingestible Knowledge capsules will wear off. Rather quickly, too."

"That's good news? I ate your jelly beans!"

"I know. This was one of those good news/bad news scenarios I have heard so much about. I, like many, decided to go with the good news first. Rejoice, my friend. You don't have to worry about Hubert Huxley being smarter than you. Well, not for very much longer, anyhow."

"But he was smart before he ate your IK capsules. Way smarter than I was before I ate mine."

"Well, yes. There's that. Say, why don't you drop by my lab when you are finished dealing with the agony of defeat there at the TV studio? We could go over the results of my testing in detail. After all, you're much smarter than me. For another week or so."

"A week?"

"Maybe ten days. Please come by the lab. Bring Grace and Kojo. You will need friends to help you face your coming sadness."

"Mom wants to take us all out to dinner at Motorino Pizza," he told Farooqi.

"Really? She is hosting a pizza party to celebrate your defeat at the hands of Hubert Huxley?"

"It was supposed to be a victory celebration."

"Ah. That makes much more sense. Very well. Shall we meet tomorrow after the conclusion of your school day?"

"I could skip school. Call in sick."

"No, Subject One. That is not advisable. Once the jelly beans wear off, you are going to need a good education more than ever. Unless, of course, working together, we rectify my mistakes and create the new and improved IK capsules! But that will take time. On the bright side, I am glad we discovered this design flaw before we went wide with mass distribution of my breakthrough creation."

Right, thought Jake. *I'm the only one who has to suffer the consequences of Farooqi's mistakes.*

Well, me and Hubert.

And Hubert doesn't know he's going to lose his "Captain Brainiac" superpowers almost as quickly as he found them.

50

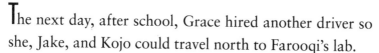

The next day, after school, Grace hired another driver so she, Jake, and Kojo could travel north to Farooqi's lab.

"We'll hold your hand the whole time," said Kojo.

Jake wished Grace had been the one to say that.

"Hey," said Grace, "even if the jelly beans do wear off, you'll still be you, Jake."

"And probably a whole lot more fun," muttered Kojo under his breath.

"Welcome, welcome, welcome!" said Farooqi when the three friends stepped into his lab. "Please. Find a seat. There are some buried underneath those stacks of paper. I think. I know I used to have chairs in here. Somewhere."

"Found one," said Grace.

"Me too," said Kojo, scooping up a load of file folders.

Jake found his seat last.

Were the jelly beans already fading? Was he losing his keen search abilities? Wait a second—did he ever really have those?

"Thank you all for joining me this afternoon," said Farooqi when everybody was finally seated. He stared at a shimmering slip of cardboard he held in his hands.

He shook his head.

"I do not like these numbers," he said solemnly.

He showed his visitors his lottery ticket.

"But the Quick Picks computer in the delicatessen selected them for me, so what am I to do but hope they are the proper combination to win the Powerball this Saturday?"

Jake threw up both arms in frustration. "What about your jelly bean research? What about those numbers?"

"Oh, of course," said Farooqi. "That is *soooo* much more important than me having the winning lottery numbers this weekend."

"Well, for me it kind of is."

"Because you have already won the lottery. Finding buried treasure. Surviving Genius Camp. Setting me up in this nice cushy lab with a hefty paycheck." He paused. "Oh. I suppose I have already won the lottery as well. Forgive my grumpiness. I drank too much tea today. Despite what you might've heard or read, some teas do indeed have caffeine."

"It's okay," said Grace. "We're all a little tense."

"Especially Jake," said Kojo with a whistle. "He's tighter than spandex on a beluga whale."

"Can we review your findings?" said Jake.

"Of course, Subject One," said Mr. Farooqi. "Of course."

Farooqi clasped his hands behind his back and paced back and forth.

"As you know, I have spent much time analyzing the only knowledge-boosting capsule still in my possession."

"The one you found in your plastic-bag briefcase," said Kojo.

"Yes. That one."

"Which batch was it from?" asked Grace. "The first, second, or third?"

"Exactly. We have no way of knowing until I learn how to paint them like M&M's. But there has been, fingers crossed, a consistency among all three iterations of my IK capsules. Now then . . ."

He held up a tweezer clutching the squished and mangled remains of the splotchy, speckled bean.

"This particular pellet has really been put through the wringer. And the spectral scanner. And my gas chromatography equipment—which I also employ on Taco Tuesdays. I even did this thing with the Bunsen burner that melted some of the splotches into squiggles."

"What flavor is that bean?" asked Grace.

"Tutti-frutti."

"From the Italian *tutti i frutti* meaning 'all the fruits,' " said Jake. "A colorful confection containing various candied fruits or an artificial flavoring simulating that taste, as in tutti-frutti ice cream."

"Correct, Subject One!" said Farooqi merrily. "You've still got it."

"Yeah, but for how long?" said Kojo.

"My best projection?" Farooqi gazed at the mangled jelly bean clenched in the stainless-steel pincers as if it were a seriously ill friend. "As I told you last night. One week. Maybe ten days."

"I'm really going to lose my superpowers? I won't be a genius anymore?"

Farooqi placed a comforting hand on Jake's shoulder. "I'm afraid so, my friend. Your intelligence will wear off. You will wake up one morning and, *pffft!* It will be gone."

"What about those folks from Genius Camp?" asked Kojo. "The ones who ate the marshmallows? The ones we brought back with jelly beans?"

"Oh, they should be fine," said Farooqi. "In their case, my confection simply zeroed out the effects of that other fiendish, if somewhat squishy and tasty, treat."

So that was that.

In a week, maybe ten days, he'd just be Jake McQuade.

He'd be just like everyone else who wasn't as brilliant as Grace or Kojo.

He would no longer be the smartest kid in the universe.

But, hey, maybe that wouldn't be so bad.

He could go back to knocking knuckles with his buds, hanging out in the cafeteria, playing games on his phone, cracking jokes, and pulling pranks.

He wouldn't have to worry about the great responsibilities that came with great power anymore.

Because his great powers would be all gone.

51

That same Tuesday, Hubert Huxley was traveling north with a minibus full of minions.

They were headed to New York's Adirondack Mountains. To Zane Zinkle's secret hideout.

"I have a very good idea as to why Mr. Zinkle might need two enormous diamonds," Hubert told his troops.

"Why?" asked Chauncy, the leader of the strike force he'd assembled. Eddie was behind the wheel. Amir and Betina were in the back of the van with Hubert. All of them wore black canvas coveralls with Jolly Roger pirate patches on their shoulders. They also wore black felt pirate hats and eye patches, because Hubert (also known as the pirate king Captain Brainiac) paid them a ton of money.

"I will reveal all at the appropriate time, my loyal henchpeople. But trust me, when this mission is completed, you will all see a hefty bonus in your bank accounts!"

A few hours later, the van reached Tupper Lake, New York. Captain Brainiac and his team wound their way up Hawk Ridge Road and rolled into a gravel driveway. Ten yards up the tree-lined road, they came to a stop at a security gate.

The guard there gestured for Eddie, the driver, to lower his window.

"You people lost or somethin'?" the guard asked brusquely.

Eddie jabbed a thumb over his shoulder to indicate Hubert in the second row, because he knew Captain Brainiac would be the one answering any and all questions.

"Lost?" said Hubert with a chuckle. "Hardly, my good sir." He didn't make eye contact with the guard. He was staring at his laptop screen. "You're Nikos Gataki, correct?"

The guard looked taken aback. "Maybe. Who are you?"

"Your new boss."

"Ha! What, you're going to pay me more than Dr. Doublé does?"

"That is correct, Nikos." Hubert tapped his computer. "In fact, I just tripled your salary. Go ahead. Check your banking app. We'll wait."

The man named Nikos pulled out his phone, swiped a finger up and down the screen a few times, and started smiling.

"Sweet," he said. "What's this Captain Brainiac, LLC?"

Hubert smiled. "That's me. May we please enter?"

"Sure, sure." Nikos raised the gate. "Go right on in, sir."

"Thank you. Oh, by the way, I also just tripled the salary of each of your colleagues. They all work for me now. Can you kindly inform them of my arrival?"

"You bet, boss," said Nikos, reaching for his walkie-talkie. "But what about Dr. Doublé?"

"In time she will also join my team, and together we will complete what I suspect is a major deal she's been pursuing for some time now."

"And Mr. Zinkle?"

Hubert's grin grew wider. "He will be out of the picture. Completely. Onward, Eddie. To the cottage. Zane Zinkle and I need to have a little chat before the county sheriff arrives to give him the bad news."

The van crawled up the long driveway to a rustic three-story stone-and-log cottage with enormous glass windows. The security guards waved it along.

"Thanks for the raise, Captain Brainiac!" shouted one.

"And the bonus!" shouted another.

All the members of the Consortium who had escaped Liberty Island with Dr. Doublé and Zane Zinkle were now firmly in Hubert's hip pocket. It was amazing how much loyalty money could buy.

The van pulled to a stop at the steps leading up to a screened-in porch.

Hubert unfolded his long limbs and climbed out.

"May I help you, young man?" said a woman standing on the porch.

Dr. Doublé.

"Hello, Doctor. Nice to see you again."

She gave him a puzzled look. "Have we met?"

"Not really. But I was watching when you double-crossed Jake McQuade and his nerdy friends. When you stole la Gran Calabaza for Zane Zinkle."

"I have no idea what—"

"There was a big statue behind you? Green lady in a toga holding up a torch?" He struck the pose. Dr. Doublé didn't react. He waved her off. "Never mind. But I don't think Mr. Zinkle can deliver the full potential of the weapon he's building for you without this."

Hubert jammed his hands into the pocket of his hoodie.

And pulled out the Red Lion Diamond.

52

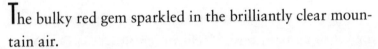

The bulky red gem sparkled in the brilliantly clear mountain air.

Dr. Doublé took one step forward and pushed open the porch's screen door.

"How did you—"

"Steal this when you couldn't? Simple. I'm smarter than the smartest kid in the universe, the doofus who set up the display case's security system. You remember Jake McQuade. If I'm not mistaken, you spent a good deal of time pretending to be interested in his talents and abilities."

Dr. Doublé looked around to make sure no one was listening. She lowered her voice. "Only so he might lure Zane Zinkle out of hiding."

"Which, hooray, he did. Mission accomplished."

Amir, Chauncy, Eddie, and Betina were standing behind Hubert now, all wearing their pirate costumes.

Hubert wanted his henchpeople to look like the ones in the comic books. One day he might even build himself a subterranean lair. In the crater of a dormant volcano. Or on an island shaped like a skull. One of those.

He'd show his father who the true evildoer in the family was. He'd show his grandmother how not-lazy he could be.

"Is Mr. Zinkle here?" asked Hubert, smoothing back his thick swoop of hair. Several of his minions cracked their knuckles.

"Frankie?" said Dr. Doublé, calling for one of *her* henchpeople. "Intruder alert."

Frankie came out onto the porch. "Sorry, Doc. I work for Captain Brainiac, LLC, now." He held up his phone. "Can you believe this benefits package?"

"I know," said Amir. "Medical *and* dental."

Hubert grinned at Dr. Doublé, who'd just realized that all her employees and underlings were now Captain Brainiac's employees and underlings.

"How about we all work together?" said Dr. Doublé with a very pleasant smile.

"Fine," said Hubert. He would string her along. He really didn't need the money from her client. But he wanted what Zane Zinkle was attempting to build. His superweapon. Every supervillain needed a superweapon. "So how are things progressing?"

"Wonderfully well," said Dr. Doublé. "I think our client will be very, very pleased."

Her eyelid was twitching. She was lying. Zane Zinkle hadn't been able to deliver.

"Marvelous," said Hubert. He made for the cabin door. Frankie held it open for him.

"After you, Captain Brainiac."

"Thank you, Frankie."

Hubert entered the mammoth lodge and strolled across its grand foyer.

And there he was. In the lower living room.

Noise-canceling headphones on. Uniform of black turtleneck and blue jeans in place.

The legendary Zane Zinkle was staring down at a massive blueprint spread out on the worktable in front of him. Three corners of the impressively intricate design were anchored by paperweights. Glass pine cones and pineapples. The fourth corner was held in place by a big, shimmering orange rock.

La Gran Calabaza.

53

Zinkle seemed lost in thought.

Hubert tapped him gently on the shoulder.

"Hmmm?"

Zinkle turned around. Removed his headphones.

"Who are you?"

Hubert smiled. "Your new nemesis."

"Excuse me?"

"I have replaced Jake McQuade as the smartest kid in the universe and, therefore, your biggest threat."

"Frankie?" Zinkle said to the muscle man who used to work for the Consortium. "Kindly remove this child from my workspace. I'm trying to build a superweapon. I can't do that with ridiculous distractions!"

Frankie laughed. "You offering me free dental?"

"What?"

"Frankie works for me now," said Hubert. "As do all

the former employees of the Consortium who were tasked with providing you security." He squinted down at the blueprints and tsked his tongue. "Oopsy. Major mistake there, Zanester."

"What? Where?"

"Here," said Hubert, pointing at the complicated schematic. "Your convergence point is wrong for optimal power transfer. Plus, you really need two giant diamonds to make this nightmare a reality."

Dr. Doublé stepped forward. "Can you fix it, Captain Brainiac?"

Zinkle looked confused. "That's your name?"

"Indeed it is," said Hubert.

"But you're a child. How could you be promoted to captain of anything?"

"I am a pirate captain like my ancient ancestor Aliento de Perro!" screamed Hubert. "I can make this weapon fully operational. For I have . . ." He paused for dramatic effect. "The Red Lion Diamond!"

Zinkle gasped when he heard that.

"Give it to me!" he said. "I need that gemstone!"

"I know you do." Hubert turned to his flock of flunkies. "Quickly now. Roll up these blueprints. Secure la Gran Calabaza. We have work to do, but we can't do it here."

Suddenly, from off in the distance, came the wailing of approaching sirens.

"I'm so sorry, Zane," said Hubert. "Sounds like you're about to be evicted from this lovely lakeside cottage."

"What?"

"It seems the shell corporation you created to finance your stay here in the Adirondacks has gone bankrupt and defaulted on all its loans. Your personal bank accounts under all your aliases? They're empty, too. That's why the sheriff is coming to pay you a visit."

"Impossible!"

"No, Mr. Zinkle! With Captain Brainiac, everything is possible. I suspect the authorities might also want to question you about that thing you tried with your nefarious Tweedle app. Kudos on that, by the way. It almost worked. Almost."

"I can give you money—"

"I don't need money! I have knowledge! And knowledge is much more valuable! Because knowledge is power!"

Hubert looked up toward the cathedral ceiling, raised both arms, and shook his fists. "Mwahaha!"

He smiled and lowered his arms.

"I've always wanted to do that," he said quite calmly. "Now then, Mr. Zinkle, if you still have your drone suit, you might wish to deploy it and beat a hasty retreat. NOW!"

Zinkle fled through the sliding glass door and headed down to a shed near the lake.

"Let him go!" Hubert told his flunkies. "Grab the

diamond. Dismantle the device. Roll up the plans. We're heading back to New York City. We need to complete and then test-fire this weapon at a target of my choosing. It's time Captain Brainiac showed the world—not to mention my father and my grandmother—just how much fire he has in his belly! More than a dragon! Mwahahaa!"

54

Jake stood at the window of Farooqi's lab, staring down at the sparkling moat circling the entrance to the corporate headquarters building.

"We had a good run, Subject One," said Mr. Farooqi.

"And you'll be back, baby," added Kojo. "Just as soon as Mr. Farooqi whips up another batch of beans."

"If you have trouble with your homework between now and then," added Grace, "we'll help you."

"Sure we will," said Kojo.

"You were a pretty great guy before you were a genius," said Grace. "I mean, I didn't really know you back then, but that's what people say. That's what they all told me." It was her turn to blush.

"Besides," said Kojo, trying to buck Jake up, "you still have a week, maybe even ten days. That's plenty of time to do all sorts of geniusy stuff. You can even beat me at chess a few more times. . . ."

Jake's phone started blaring a brassy spy-movie ringtone.

"It's the ODNI," Jake told his friends.

"Huh?" said Grace.

Kojo translated. "The Office of the Director of National Intelligence. Everett Robertson. The head of the whole US intelligence community."

"Oh my," said Farooqi. "I suggest you take the call, Jake. They will most certainly know if you are ghosting them."

Jake raised his phone and tapped the screen.

"Yes, Mr. Robertson?" he said.

"Are you still at Zinkle headquarters?"

"Yes, sir."

"Good. That's where your mother said we'd find you. Stand by. A chopper will be arriving at the rooftop landing pad in five. We need you down in DC."

"Really? Because it's a school night."

"This is a matter of utmost urgency, Jake. Bring Kojo and Grace along if you like."

"How'd you know they were here with me?" Jake asked.

There was a slight pause. A silence. Everett Robertson gave no reply.

"Oh right," said Jake, putting his phone into speaker mode. "You're the director of national intelligence. You know everything."

"What'd I have for lunch today?" asked Kojo.

"A peanut butter and banana sandwich you brought from home," said Robertson. "Grace had the hummus grab-and-go served in the cafeteria. Mr. Farooqi had chicken karahi. Again."

"It's true," said Farooqi. "It is quite delicious. I also like saying the name. Chicken karahi. Doesn't it just make you smile?"

"What's this all about?" Jake asked.

"Zane Zinkle. Since pulling his disappearing act at the Statue of Liberty, he's gone completely rogue. The FBI tells us Zinkle is working with the mercenary group known as the Consortium. Their leader, Dr. Marie Doublé, whom you are familiar with, is currently in possession of the world's largest orange diamond."

"Because she stole it from us," said Kojo.

"Correct," said Robertson. "We fear that she and Zinkle are now working together at a remote, unidentified location. They will use the large orange diamond to create a massive space weapon. A superlaser, which, if mounted on a hostile nation's satellite, could do serious damage to America's national security interests."

"You mean like the evil empire's ultimate weapon in *Star Wars*?" said Grace. "The Death Star?"

There was another pause. "That is our fear," said Robertson. "We think Zinkle is working with the Consortium to construct a weapon where multiple lasers are transferred into a single focused beam that can be directed at the intended target."

"An interesting hypothesis," Jake said dully, because being a genius wasn't much fun when you realized you wouldn't be a genius much longer. "The key would be a *pair* of large diamonds at the point of beam convergence, able to combine several different high-intensity lasers. The bigger the diamonds, the more powerful the laser beam."

"Just like in *Star Wars*," muttered Grace.

Jake heard the *whomp-whomp-whomp* of an approaching helicopter.

"We can discuss all of this further once you're down here in DC," said Everett Robertson.

"Marvelous!" said Farooqi. "I have always wanted to visit this nation's capital. I understand one can see the space shuttle *Discovery* as well as a folding bathtub at the Smithsonian Institution."

"Have a great time, you guys," said Jake.

"What?" said the stunned intelligence director.

"I'm not going. I'm not the person you need for this assignment, Mr. Robertson."

"We can't figure this thing out if you're not on the team, Jake!"

"Yes, you can. Just find somebody brilliant. Somebody who has all the answers, no matter the question. Don't you watch *Quiz Zone*? I'm not that person anymore. I'm just Jake McQuade."

55

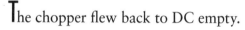

The chopper flew back to DC empty.

Everett Robertson was "seriously disappointed" in Jake.

So were Jake's friends at the FBI, CIA, DOD, and DEA. Word spread fast. Jake McQuade was out of the game. He no longer wished to be of assistance to anyone doing anything important.

He wanted to go back to being a middle school slacker.

Not that Jake ever said that. It's just what everybody heard when he told Mr. Robertson, "I'm not your guy anymore."

"Sure," said Deputy Assistant Director Don Struchen, "we know you're just a kid, Jake. But, well, we thought you were a special kid."

"I was," Jake told him over the phone. "For a little while. Now I'm just me."

After that call, Jake erased Mr. Struchen's contact information from his phone. The special hotline number he'd been given. Then he erased all his government and intelligence-agency contacts. Because in a week, maybe ten days, he wouldn't be able to help any of them.

"You know," Kojo reminded him, "you haven't lost your superpowers yet."

"You could still do a bunch of good stuff," added Grace.

"What's the point?" Jake told them both.

And—he could tell—they were both seriously disappointed in him.

Jake spent most of the next week, his last as a super-genius, eating potato chips and scrolling through photos from the good old days. Winning the Quiz Bowl regionals. Horsing around with Kojo in Mr. Farooqi's shabby basement lab at Corey Hall. Posing with Grace, the treasure chest propped open behind them like a bubbler in a fishbowl. Jake's high-tech cabin at Genius Camp. Kojo pretending to barf up a basket of chocolate-covered marshmallows. Good times.

Since the jelly beans hadn't worn off completely, Jake did spend a couple of hours every day after school tutoring people who were having trouble with their homework.

Catch me while I still know the answers, Jake thought. *It's our final big blowout sale. Everything must go before it's all gone for good.*

He actually enjoyed helping his classmates understand

stuff, like how to calculate the volume of a sphere with a radius of two centimeters. It was the highlight of his day.

Maybe because Kojo and Grace were right there with him.

"Jake?" said Kojo, sounding weirdly philosophical after all their tutees had gone home. "Remember: nothing lasts forever, baby. Except maybe plastic bags."

"And change," said Grace. "That's a constant. Everything keeps changing."

"And energy," said Jake, ready for one last brainy burst. "As we know from thermodynamics . . ."

"Here we go," said Kojo with a chuckle.

"Tell us more, oh wise professor," said Grace.

Oh, what the heck, thought Jake. *I might as well. For old times' sake.*

"Energy cannot be created nor destroyed. It simply changes states. Of course, we also know from Einstein that matter and energy are inexorably entwined."

Kojo threw up his hands. "When are these jelly beans gonna wear off?" He checked his watch. "I'm hoping it's sometime soon. Real soon."

Jake couldn't help it. When Grace laughed at Kojo's joke, he found himself laughing along with her.

Maybe Kojo was right. Nothing lasted forever. But it had been fun. He'd enjoyed the ride. And the helicopter rides. And working with the FBI. And the proud look in his mother's eyes. And helping Grace find her family's buried treasure. Twice!

Jake looked at Kojo and Grace and said something he felt more strongly than anything he'd ever felt before.

"Thanks, you guys. For everything."

"You're welcome," said Grace.

"De nada," said Kojo.

On the tenth day after Haazim Farooqi made his prognosis about Jake's superintelligence fading away, Grace brought three homemade cupcakes to the cafeteria where they were going to do their final homework-help session together.

The cupcakes were chocolate with white frosting. One had glittering sprinkles shaped into a crude *J* on top.

"That's yours," Grace told Jake. "For later."

After an hour of solving algebra, discussing Newton's laws of motion, and exploring the Bill of Rights, the trio of tutors said goodbye to their classmates.

"Kojo and Grace will still be able to help you tomorrow," Jake told his final student, Caroline Bolt. "Me? Not so much."

"How come?" asked Caroline.

"Remember that, uh, mental growth spurt I had a while back?"

"Sure. It was weird. One day you couldn't spell 'rudimentary' on a vocabulary test. The next you were explaining to the teacher that it came from a Latin word meaning 'rough, crude, or unlearned.' "

"Yeah," said Jake. " 'Rudis.' The same Latin word that gave us 'rude.' "

"Then you belched to illustrate your point."

Jake nodded. "Good times, Caroline. Good times. Anyhow, they say I might go into a slump soon."

"Like a baseball player who hits a bunch of home runs and then can't do anything but strike out?" said Caroline.

"Yeah. Like that."

He couldn't've said it better himself.

56

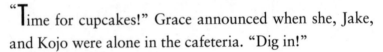

"Time for cupcakes!" Grace announced when she, Jake, and Kojo were alone in the cafeteria. "Dig in!"

She handed Jake his cupcake.

He smiled and took a big chomp.

And spit it right out.

Because the white vanilla frosting? It was actually mayonnaise.

"Gotcha!" said Grace.

"Revenge is a dish best served cold, baby," said Kojo. "Cold and slimy."

Jake grabbed a napkin to wipe the cake crumbs and mayo off his lips and chin. Then he grabbed another one to scrub his tongue.

"Good one, Grace," he said. "You got me. And you guys are right. Sure, I'll miss being the guy who figures out a theory in four-dimensional space-time that includes interactions without resorting to perturbative methods, but it'll be fun to be me again. The Jake McQuade who'll prank you back when you least expect it."

They headed out of the cafeteria.

"I'm definitely not looking forward to April Fools' Day this year," Grace said with a laugh.

"Oh, I am," said Jake. "By the way, did you guys know that some historians say April Fools' Day dates back to Geoffrey Chaucer and his fourteenth-century collection *The Canterbury Tales,* where he jokes about the thirty-second day of March, which, of course, would be April first?"

"No," said Kojo. "I did not know that. Neither did anybody else."

"The day is also linked to the vernal equinox, the first day of spring in the Northern Hemisphere, when Mother Nature fooled people with unpredictable weather."

"Uh, Jake?" said Kojo.

Jake wasn't done. "In Scotland, the pranks go on for two whole days. April second is Tailie Day, when cele-brants traditionally attach a paper tail or a 'kick me' sign to their friends' bahoochies, which, of course, is what they call butts in Scotland."

"Where are you getting all this?" asked Grace.

Jake shrugged. "Must be the jelly beans."

"Hold up," said Kojo. "I thought you were supposed to lose all that today."

"Farooqi gave us his best guess. An estimate, which,

as you know from math class, means a value close enough to the right answer, usually arrived at with some thought or calculation. I'm actually thinking about pursuing a career where I estimate crowd sizes at outdoor events."

Grace and Kojo both gave him a puzzled look.

Jake just nodded. "I wonder how many people there are in that field?"

It took a second, but Jake's friends realized it was a joke.

Grace shook her head. "Funny *and* smart," she said as the three friends started walking again. "I like that."

Yeah, thought Jake. *I'd like that, too. Who says you have to always be serious when you're smart? Why can't it be fun, too?*

If Mr. Farooqi ever did recreate his incredible IK jelly beans, Jake would ask for a do-over. One where he put a little less pressure on himself.

The three friends exited the building and headed up the block.

Jake saw them first.

"You guys? Get down!"

Jake hid behind a mailbox. Grace and Kojo ducked behind a boxy, solar-powered garbage compacting bin.

"What is it?" whispered Kojo.

"Across the street," said Jake. "That moving van. See it?"

Several beefy bodybuilder types in black jumpsuits

and what looked like pirate hats were hauling wooden crates down the truck's ramp with a rolling pallet jack.

"That's Frankie," Jake whispered. "From the Consortium."

"Those others are the people who stole la Gran Calabaza from us on Liberty Island," said Grace.

"Why are they in pirate costumes?" wondered Kojo. "Is it Halloween somewhere?"

"Careful with that, you boneheaded lummox!" someone shouted.

Hubert Huxley.

"That's precious cargo. Transport it upstairs immediately. Grandmama's penthouse is all ours. I sent her on a cruise to the Bahamas!"

"You heard Captain Brainiac," said a woman wearing a headscarf and big dark sunglasses.

She spoke with a thick French accent.

Because she was Dr. Doublé!

57

"My place," Jake whispered. "Take separate routes. Meet in the lobby. Go."

Kojo headed down the block. Grace headed up it. Jake took the cross street east. He figured they would be less noticeable if they weren't traveling in a pack.

Fifteen minutes later, they reconvened in the lobby of Jake's apartment building.

"What's going on?" Grace asked. "Why are those criminals moving into the apartment building across the street from our school?"

"And why is Hubert Huxley with them?" wondered Kojo. "Is he trying to swap the red diamond he stole for the orange diamond *they* stole?"

"I don't think so," said Jake, his brain buzzing. He had a suspicion. One he hoped wasn't true. "They have *both* diamonds. They might be working on that space laser everybody warned us about. They might've already started construction. That could be what's inside all those crates."

"So where's Zane Zinkle?" asked Grace.

"Maybe he's already inside the building."

"You mean 92 Riverside Drive?" said Kojo. "That's right. I made a note of it. Took a few snapshots, too. Why? Because that's what sleuths do, baby."

"Good work!" said Grace.

"Come on," said Jake. "We need to figure out a plan."

Jake, Grace, and Kojo took the elevator up to Jake's floor and hurried into his apartment.

"Hi, guys," said Jake's mom. "Anybody hungry? We have some shrimp bisque in the fridge that Jake whipped up over the weekend."

Kojo crinkled his nose. "Is that like fish soup?"

"I typically serve it as a first course," said Jake modestly.

"Not right now, Ms. McQuade," said Grace. "We had a snack at school. Cupcakes with yummy vanilla frosting."

Jake urped a little when Grace said that.

"We've got a homework project we need to work on," said Kojo.

"Does this project have anything to do with the FBI, buried treasure, or Zane Zinkle?" asked Ms. McQuade.

"No," said Jake, his voice cracking slightly. It happened every time he told his mom a fib.

"Then have fun."

"Thanks, Mom."

Jake led his friends down the hall to his room.

He sat at his homework desk, slid out the keyboard tray, and started tapping in search parameters. "I want to cross-reference the name Huxley with 92 Riverside Drive."

It took Google less than a second to come up with the answer.

"Mrs. Penelope Flippington Huxley, mother of disgraced real estate tycoon Heath Huxley, bought the twenty-second-floor penthouse apartment in that building ten years ago."

Jake clacked more keys.

"These real estate websites are amazing. They've got floor plans for every apartment in that building. Here's the penthouse. It's right across the street from Riverview Middle School."

Jake leaned back in his rolling chair.

"I wish there was some way for us to find out what those guys from the Consortium are doing up there with Hubert Huxley."

"We should call your friends at the FBI," said Grace.

"Not yet," said Jake. "We need to gather more intelligence. For all we know, those big wooden crates just have home-entertainment equipment inside them."

"But how do we gather that intelligence?" said Kojo. "A fancy apartment building like that is going to have tight

226

security. Doorpeople. Cameras everywhere. We can't just drop by, pretend we're selling Girl Scout cookies, and take a peek inside Mrs. Huxley's apartment." Kojo paused. "Unless. We could do awesome disguises like they do on *Mission: Impossible*. Those latex masks. We just need to buy a couple boxes of cookies at the deli. Find some wigs. Some Girl Scout uniforms. Make rubber masks—"

"Or," said Grace, pointing at the penthouse floor plan, "we could take a peek through these front windows."

"Um, we'd need a crane to do that," said Jake.

"Or a big friendly giant," said Kojo. "Like the one in that Roald Dahl book."

"Or . . . ," Grace added, "a drone with a camera."

Jake and Kojo both tilted their heads sideways like curious puppies.

"Okay," said Grace. "Fine. A closetful of kicks wasn't all I bought with my treasure money. I also picked up a two-axis gimbal quadcopter drone with a 4K camera and HD video transmission."

Jake and Kojo nodded.

"Cool," said Kojo.

"Super cool," said Jake. "Can you bring it to school tomorrow?"

58

The next day, Grace, Jake, and Kojo got a permission slip from Mr. Lyons to conduct "gutter inspection research" during their lunch period.

"We spent so much money fixing up the inside of this school," said Grace, "we really need to stay on top of any potential water-damage issues up on the roof."

"If those gutters are clogged," said Kojo, "we could get leaks."

"Especially in the winter," added Jake. "If stagnant water trapped by leaves freezes, ice dams will form along the ridge of the roof. As it melts and freezes and remelts and refreezes, that ice could create intense pressure under the lip of the roofing surface, pry open cracks, and generate leaks."

Mr. Lyons was impressed by their initiative. And by how much Jake knew about gutters and ice.

"Let me know what you find out," he said.

Jake and Kojo went out to Riverside Drive with Grace.

She commanded her four-propellor drone to lift off gently from the sidewalk. It rose straight up, like a helicopter. Then, after it had climbed the six stories to the roof, she had it hover there. The drone's camera beamed down a crystal-clear image that was recorded on a small handheld device.

"You can tilt the camera with those controls," Grace explained to Jake, who'd handle the camera work while she flew the drone. "If you want to zoom in, just stretch your fingers on the glass screen like you would on your phone."

"Got it," said Jake.

"The new water tank is looking good," said Kojo when Grace made the drone pass by the giant wooden barrel on stilts. "And there's that Frisbee I lost in sixth grade! How'd it get way up there?"

"Let's worry about that later," said Grace.

"Sure, sure. I can make a sacrifice for the greater good."

"Okay, Grace," said Jake, "I've got the hang of the camera. Let's zip it across the street."

Grace thumbed the dual joystick controllers and expertly drifted the drone on a diagonal to the towering apartment building.

"Elevating," she said, sounding like a NASA engineer

in mission control. "Geomagnetic calibration holding steady. Gimbals adjusting to wind flow."

Jake kept his eyes glued to the video screen.

"Can you get any closer to the window? There's something going on in the living room. Near the grand piano."

"Vectoring drone toward glass," said Grace.

"Steady, steady," coached Kojo, probably because people said that a lot on TV shows.

"They're building something," Jake reported. "They have a spherical skeleton set up. And, yes—they have both diamonds! I can see them!"

"Is Zane Zinkle in there?" gasped Kojo, peering over Jake's shoulder. "Is he making a Death Star laser beam?"

"No. I mean, Zinkle isn't in there. But, yes, it does look like they're working with multiple lasers. Lots of 'em. Hubert is staring at a schematic. Now he's screaming at Dr. Doublé. He's not happy. Dr. Doublé looks upset, too. Hubert just yanked the plug. The lasers all went dark. Quick, Grace. Lower the drone! Fast."

Grace flicked her joysticks. The drone dropped down a few floors.

"Turn around and point at the school, you guys!" said Jake.

His friends did.

"Why are we pointing at the school?" asked Kojo.

"Because I'm pretty sure Hubert Huxley is up in the corner window of that penthouse glaring down at us!"

"Well," said Kojo, "let's give him something to glare at."

He held up his phone and started dancing.

"Not this again," muttered Grace.

"Relax," said Kojo. "This time, it's just for TikTok."

59

Once they were back inside the school, Jake, Kojo, and Grace headed to the library.

It was always a great place to think. And they still had ten minutes left in their lunch period.

"We should definitely call the FBI," said Grace.

Jake agreed. He also wished he hadn't erased Deputy Assistant Director Don Struchen's contact information from his phone.

"I trashed all my contacts," he said. "FBI, CIA, DOD."

"Well, that wasn't very smart," said Kojo. "Guess those jelly beans really are wearing off."

"They're up there in that penthouse building a Death Star," Grace whispered so intensely her voice squeaked. "We have to tell somebody!"

"The cloud!" Jake exclaimed.

"What?" said Kojo.

Jake dashed over to the nearest computer. "My contacts are all backed up in the cloud. I just need to sign in to my account and click restore." He rolled the mouse and made all the right clicks. "We're back in business!"

He speed-dialed Mr. Struchen.

"This is a special number they gave me," Jake told his friends. "My own private hotline."

"We are sorry, Mr. McQuade," said a recorded voice. "This number has been disconnected and is no longer in service. If you feel you have reached this recording in error, please check the number and try your call again."

Jake tried again.

All he got was the same recorded message.

He tried six more times. Nothing.

The same thing happened when Jake called the special hotline numbers he had for his spy friends and the generals he'd helped at the Pentagon.

"They've all blocked me," he said.

"Can you blame them?" said Kojo. "Face it, Jake, you quit on them. Threw in the towel. Raised the white flag. Said, 'Gotta go, Buffalo.'"

Jake knew Kojo was right. But could he fix it?

"How about the police?" he said. "We could show them the tape from the drone."

"It's illegally obtained evidence," said Grace. "We were spying. We didn't have permission to peep inside that penthouse."

"She's right," said Kojo. "We'd be laughed out of

court. But first we'd be laughed out of the police station. How about Principal Lyons?"

Grace shook her head. "Uncle Charley's not here. He had a lunch meeting downtown with the chancellor of the Department of Education."

"Niiiice," said Kojo.

Suddenly, a voice came over the school's PA system.

"Jake McQuade, Grace Garcia, and Kojo Shelton. Please report to the principal's office."

60

Jake looked at Kojo and Grace.

They both had *Huh?* looks on their faces. Jake did, too.

"Let's go see what's up," he said.

"Beats sitting here getting nowhere except closer to a headache," said Kojo.

"Totally," said Grace.

They made their way to Mr. Lyons's office.

There was a snooty-looking elderly lady sitting in a visitor chair. Her back was as stiff as a slab of stale bubble gum. Her face was puckered into a scowl.

A man in a chauffeur uniform stood beside her.

The woman rose from her seat the instant Jake, Kojo, and Grace entered the office.

"You three need to come with me," she proclaimed. "Immediately."

"Um, why?" said Grace. "We don't even know you."

"Stranger danger," sang Kojo.

The stern lady ignored Kojo and kept her gaze focused on Grace.

"You may not know me, Miss Garcia, but I know you. In fact, I am a fan."

"That's very nice but—"

"Pay attention, young lady. I am 'A Fan.' The person who recently sent you an anonymous note." She lowered her voice. "¿Las tres hermanas ostras?"

"That was you?"

"Yes. For goodness' sake, clean the wax out of your ears. I just said that."

"Who exactly are you?" demanded Jake.

"I am Penelope Flippington Huxley. This is Chauncy, my driver. I believe you three know my grandson, Hubert?"

"We've met," said Kojo.

Mrs. Huxley curled her lip into a snarl.

"How would you children like to have tea with me in my penthouse across the street? I think you'll find it very . . . *rewarding.*"

"Quick question," said Kojo. "Why, exactly, are you inviting us to this impromptu tea party?"

"Because," said Mrs. Huxley, "you three have, in the past, defeated my son and my grandson for your own nefarious purposes."

"The Quiz Bowl wasn't all that nefarious," said Grace defensively.

Mrs. Huxley ignored her. "This time, I need you to defeat Hubert for *me*! He has fallen in with the wrong crowd. Under their influence, he has stolen something that doesn't belong solely to him." She lowered her voice. "¡La Gran Calabaza!"

Jake looked to Grace and Kojo.

They both nodded.

They all agreed.

With the luxury building's tight security, Mrs. Huxley was probably their only way in. They'd figure out next steps after they finished this first one.

"Mrs. Duggan?" Jake said to the brand-new school secretary, who'd just returned to her desk from the copy machine.

"Yes, Jake?"

"We, uh, need to head across the street. To 92 Riverside Drive."

"It's urgent," said Grace.

"They need us up in the penthouse apartment," added Kojo, probably because it sounded cool.

Mrs. Duggan, who'd just started at Riverview Middle, was already used to Jake, Grace, and Kojo leaving school for unusual reasons.

"If the FBI calls," she joked, "I'll tell them where to find you."

Jake knew the FBI wouldn't be calling. The three friends were on their own.

61

"**A**im it at the water tank on top of the school, you dolts!" Hubert commanded his minions.

But they weren't listening to him.

"Hello? I gave you an order! Push that Death Star contraption over here and point it at the big wooden tank. We're going to dunk them! We'll flood the top floor. It'll be our warning shot fired across the bow of the world. Then we'll take this superweapon to my pirate yacht and flee to the high seas. Arrr!"

"This weapon is supposed to be sold to the highest bidder," said Dr. Doublé. "They will mount it on a satellite, send it up into space, and terrorize their neighbors."

"I might do that, too!" said Hubert. "But first I'm going to punk Riverview Middle School. My father will be so proud of me. He wanted to tear that school down.

I bet the city will do it after the building floods. Yes! We strike tonight. When the place is empty! Quickly! Move it over here and aim it at that wooden water tank so it'll be ready!"

Nobody obeyed his orders.

"Where's Chauncy?" Hubert demanded. "He's been on my payroll the longest."

"That's the thing, kid," said Amir. "Your pay hasn't been rolling into our accounts the way it used to."

"Yeah," said Nikos. "And that medical and dental insurance you promised. What happened to that, 'Captain Brainiac'?"

Hubert grabbed at his bushy hair with both hands and wished he could yank it all out. Maybe that would wake up his brain.

For the past few days, he'd felt sluggish. He'd been having trouble thinking and scheming and coming up with deviously diabolical plots. He'd also forgotten everything he used to know about manipulating stock trades and wiring money to people's bank accounts. He kept having brain farts.

"Besides," said Betina, "what's the use of laser-beam blasting the school's water tank in the middle of the night?"

"It'll make a big splash!" shouted Frankie.

"Huh?" said Hubert.

"It's water. Get it? A big *splash*?"

"Is that supposed to be funny?"

"Yeah."

"Well, it isn't!"

"You know what else isn't funny?" said a stressed Dr. Doublé. "This weapon. It's still not fully operational."

"It's powerful enough to blast the water tank."

"Because it's right across the street!"

Hubert shrugged. "Hey. It's a start."

"It needs to work in outer space."

"It will," said Hubert. "Soon. I just need to adjust my miscalculations slightly."

Dr. Doublé shook her head. "What has happened to you, Hubert? You used to be so very brilliant. Was it all a charade?"

Hubert had a brief panic attack.

He didn't know how to play charades. Nobody had ever taught him.

"Does anybody have any candy?" he asked, not knowing why he was asking it. "Jelly beans, perhaps? Malted milk balls? How about Smarties? Smarties would be good."

"How about breath mints?" suggested Frankie.

I'm imploding, thought Hubert. *Or is it exploding? Which one is in and which one is out?*

Nothing was making any sense.

The whozeewhatzits he'd gobbled down weren't working anymore.

Hubert was confused. His memory was slipping.

Had he really gotten smarter by eating some kind of candy?

No. That would be impossible.

Now everybody in his grandmother's penthouse was staring at him.

"Why are you all gawking at me?"

"Because, 'Captain Brainiac,'" said Frankie, "you don't seem to be so brainy no more."

62

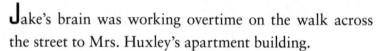

Jake's brain was working overtime on the walk across the street to Mrs. Huxley's apartment building.

He was focused on the tutti-frutti jelly bean. The only one in the bottom of that plastic shopping bag Mr. Farooqi used for a briefcase. So far the genius inventor had created three batches of IK (or KI) capsules. That meant there was a 33.3 percent chance that the tutti-frutti was a bean from the first batch, the ones Jake ate. And a 33.3 percent chance that it had come from the latest series, the ones Hubert Huxley stole. The other option was that it was a leftover from the Genius Camp bunch.

It had been more than ten days. Jake's jelly bean–enhanced brain was still buzzing. Sure, every now and then it skipped a beat. But he still knew so much.

For instance, Riverside Park, just off Riverside Drive, was once home to more goats than people. In fact,

Gotham, a nickname for New York City long before *Batman* was created, actually meant "goat's town" in Anglo-Saxon.

Yeah, his jelly bean–boosted brain seemed to be okay.

So maybe, just maybe, Hubert Huxley was the one who'd eaten the bad beans.

That meant Jake might be able to best him in some kind of impromptu *Quiz Zone*–type competition. A rematch. They could take one of those "Are You a Genius?" tests on YouTube. The winner would go home with both the diamonds. The loser would have their memories and a lifetime of regrets.

But would Hubert agree to it?

It was worth a shot.

Besides, it was the only idea Jake had. He hadn't expected Mrs. Huxley to show up at school and invite Jake, Kojo, and Grace over to her place for "tea."

They reached the apartment building.

The doorpeople waved Mrs. Huxley right in. (They looked terrified of her.)

Jake, Grace, Kojo, Mrs. Huxley, and Chauncy stepped into the cramped wood-paneled elevator.

"My ungrateful grandson is upstairs doing something preposterous with both of our diamonds," Mrs. Huxley sniffed as the elevator began its ascent to the twenty-second floor.

The floor indicator clicked from 1 to 2 to 3 very, very slowly. It was an old building. An old elevator.

"Hubert has somehow gotten his paws on both la Gran Calabaza and the lesser gemstone you children called the Red Lion. The one you had on display back there in your school lobby."

"Both those diamonds belong to my family," Grace told Mrs. Huxley.

"We can discuss custody issues later, Miss Garcia. For now we must focus on retrieving our valuables, wouldn't you agree?"

Grace hesitated, then nodded.

"Do you know what Hubert's doing with those diamonds?" asked Jake.

"Yes," said Mrs. Huxley. "I believe he and his foul new friends have constructed some sort of super laser-beam blaster."

"Like the one from *Star Wars*," said Chauncy.

"Why'd they build it here?" asked Jake. "Why not in a high-tech lab?"

"Actually," said Mrs. Huxley, "from what Chauncy tells me, they did do the preliminary work in a top-secret facility upstate."

"That's right," said Chauncy. "Then we hauled it down here."

"Why?" wondered Jake aloud.

"Oh, Hubert means well, I suppose," said Mrs. Huxley. "He wants to fulfill his father's dream. He still thinks he can get the city to condemn your school building."

"What?!"

"It's been completely refurbished," said Grace.

"Yeah," said Chauncy. "But there might be a flood. Up on the top floor."

"Excuse me," said Kojo. "Floods usually take place down on the ground floor or in the basement because, hello, that's where the water is."

"Not if a ten-thousand-gallon water tank explodes up on the roof," said Chauncy. "That's gonna be Captain Brainiac's first target."

"Right," said Jake. "He's 'Captain Brainiac' now."

Mrs. Huxley rolled her eyes. "I'm afraid so. In my opinion, the boy reads far too many comic books. Anyhow, after Hubert pulls his water-tank prank, he and his new 'business associates' will use that blast as an advertisement for the weapon's potential and sell it to the highest bidder."

"We were gonna put the laser blaster on Captain Brainiac's pirate yacht," said Chauncy. "The *Stinky Dog Two*. Then we'd sail out to international waters where the feds can't touch us and make a deal with one dictator or another. Several countries are eager to bid on our Death Star. There'll be more once the captain gives them that little demo up on the roof of your school."

Mrs. Huxley sniffed dismissively. "I, of course, was strongly opposed to the whole idea. It will take years for the city to tear down that school building. Even longer for Hubert to put up a high-rise condominium tower. That kind of construction will be noisy and dusty and frightfully inconvenient. When I raised my concerns, Hubert had me hauled off to a cruise ship. Fortunately, Chauncy was willing to listen to reason and switch sides. I'm happy to report that he once again works for me."

"We came to an understanding," said Chauncy. "I get ten percent of the Big Pumpkin Diamond. That's a hefty chunk of change."

The elevator crept up to the penthouse floor.

"Finally," said Mrs. Huxley. "Thankfully, I have my own private elevator entrance."

The door slid open.

They stepped into the foyer.

"Hello?" said Mrs. Huxley. "Hubert? Where are you, you oafish buffoon?"

No one answered.

The apartment was empty.

63

Five minutes earlier, as the team of henchpeople finished packing the laser blaster into its custom rolling crate, Dr. Doublé stood at the corner penthouse window, keeping an eye on the sidewalk below.

She saw Chauncy exit the school building with Mrs. Huxley, Grace Garcia, Kojo Shelton, and, of course, Jake McQuade.

"Traitor," she hissed.

Then she turned to the others.

"We have to leave now!"

All of Hubert Huxley's minions (minus Chauncy), plus the former employees of the Consortium, had signed on to work for Dr. Doublé. Mostly because Hubert had seemingly forgotten how to transfer money into their bank accounts.

Now the boy who called himself Captain Brainiac sat slumped in a chair.

It looked like he might be nodding off into a nap.

He snorted a loud, open-mouth snore.

"Woof," said Betina, the woman with a snake tattoo wrapped around her neck. "That kid's breath is so bad, I look forward to his farts."

Frankie snapped shut the final latch of the weapon's foam-lined carrier.

"We are good to go, Doc," he reported.

"Then let's go!" shouted Dr. Doublé. "Now! I want to be on the yacht ASAP. We'll go out to international waters. Video a demonstration of the device's power."

"You don't want to blow up the water tank across the street?" asked Amir.

"Of course not. It will draw too much unwanted attention. The local authorities will swoop in and confiscate everything. No. We leave the city and take our high-tech weapon out to the high seas!"

"What about the kid?" asked Frankie.

"Bring him along. Perhaps Hubert will, somehow, regain his superintelligence. We still need someone with an Einsteinian grasp of physics to help us refine the weapon's trajectory settings."

Two of the other goons hoisted Hubert up out of his seat.

"Eenie, meanie, jelly beanie," Hubert mumbled as he

was frog-marched out the door. He seemed to be sound asleep.

Good, thought Dr. Doublé. *Maybe young Mr. Huxley just needs a nap to regain his incredible mental prowess. Because we can't make this weapon work the way it must without some genius-level assistance!*

Dr. Doublé's muscle team trundled the space weapon and the sleepwalking Hubert onto the service elevator.

When they reached the ground floor, they quickly made their way through Riverside Park and over to the river. They boarded Hubert's superyacht, which was docked at the nearby boat basin. The luxury ship was easy to locate. It had a Jolly Roger pirate flag.

Hubert was given a comfy bed in one of the cabins.

The laser blaster was uncrated in the yacht's party room, which opened onto the deck at the stern of the ship. Frankie and Amir set the device up on the hardwood dance floor, right underneath the mirror ball in the ceiling. They hooked it up to a battery the size of a footlocker and waited for it to whir to life. Then they helped themselves to peanuts and potato chips at the party-room snack bar.

Betina, who'd actually piloted a pirate ship off the coast of Thailand, was up in the yacht's cockpit.

Dr. Doublé gave the command, and the yacht puttered out into the Hudson River.

"Laying a course for open waters," said Betina.

"Stay at a safe speed until we pass the Statue of Liberty and exit the harbor," said Dr. Doublé.

"Aye, aye, Cap'n," said Betina with a half-hearted salute. Pirates weren't big on saluting.

Dr. Doublé and her crew would slip out of the city. Down the Hudson, through New York Harbor, and out into the Atlantic Ocean. That was where they'd use their encrypted satellite phones to make an illegal offshore deal.

They would be seafaring pirates.

Just like Capitán Aliento de Perro—the original Dog Breath.

64

Jake, Kojo, and Grace made a quick sweep of all the rooms in the penthouse.

They were empty.

"Looks like they went with plan B," said Chauncy.

"Which is?" said Kojo.

"To put the Death Star thingamabob on Hubert's yacht and sail it out to international waters."

"That's twelve miles, or nineteen-point-three kilometers, offshore," said Jake.

"Well," said Grace, "we have to stop them before they get that far. They have our diamonds!"

"They, uh, also have some kind of laser-beam death ray," Kojo reminded her.

Jake turned to Chauncy. "Where did Hubert dock his ship?"

Chauncy nudged his head to the west. "Over at

the boat basin. Seventy-Ninth Street and the Hudson River."

"I know the place," said Grace. "Uncle Charley and I chartered a three-hour cruise on a sailboat there for his birthday."

"Well," said Jake, "let's hope that boat is available to rent again."

"Why?" asked Kojo. "This isn't your birthday, is it? I was going to get you a cupcake. With real vanilla icing this time . . ."

"Thanks, Kojo. But it's not my birthday. We just need to rent a boat to chase after Hubert's yacht!"

"You can't miss it," said Chauncy. "There's a pirate flag flying off the stern. Oh, and the name is painted on the hull. The *Stinky Dog Two*."

"He named it after Aliento de Perro's pirate ship!" said Grace.

"Hey," Jake said to Grace, "your ancestor was the original captain of that ship."

"True."

"So," said Kojo, "let's go stage another mutiny!"

"Hey, kids," said Chauncy. "I get ten percent of the orange diamond, remember? Mrs. Huxley here promised."

"Indeed I did," said Mrs. Huxley, who was fussing with a teapot and sugar lumps.

"We'll talk," said Grace.

The three friends hurried back onto the elevator

and punched the button for the lobby. Mrs. Huxley and Chauncy sat down to sip their tea.

The elevator door eventually crawled shut.

The car lurched a little. And shuddered.

Finally it began its long, slow descent down from the twenty-second floor.

"Where's a high-speed bullet elevator when you need one?" groused Kojo.

"Um, Kojo?" said Jake. "Not to be a noodge, but we can't really 'stage another mutiny,' because we're not on the crew."

"Good point. So let's just be a boarding party and shout 'yo-ho-ho' a lot. It's pirate time, baby."

A full three minutes later, they squeezed out of the elevator before its gliding doors were even fully opened. They sprinted across the marble floor.

"Hey, you kids!" shouted a uniformed doorman. "No running in the lobby!"

"Sorry," said Jake.

"We're in a bit of a rush," said Grace.

"We have to save the planet from a weapon of mass destruction!" added Kojo.

"Doesn't mean you can run in the lobby!" the doorman hollered after them.

They hit the street, dashed around the corner, and hurried into Riverside Park. They raced along the winding asphalt paths and into a tunnel that would take them under the highway known as the Henry Hudson Parkway and down to the river.

"That's the sailboat!" said Grace, pointing to what Jake instantly knew was a thirty-eight-foot sloop. "That's the one we rented for Uncle Charley's birthday. Come on."

As they sprinted toward the dock, Jake peered downriver.

There, not too far away, maybe half a mile, was a fancy superyacht with a pirate flag flapping in the breeze. Hubert was moving slowly. Probably so he and his boat didn't attract too much attention.

At the rental-boat pier, a man in a sweat-stained Yankees baseball cap was polishing the brass ring around a porthole, making it gleam in the sun.

"Hey there, Captain Grumby!" shouted Grace.

The man squinted at her. "Do I know you?"

"You took her and her uncle Charley on a sailboat ride for his birthday," said Kojo.

"Three years ago," added Grace.

The man took off his baseball cap and scratched his scraggly hair. "I did? Far out."

"We'd like to charter another cruise," said Jake. He pointed at the yacht flying the Jolly Roger. "We need to follow that pirate ship."

"Pirate ship?"

"Well, they have the flag. . . ."

"Hey, you're that kid. From TV. *Quiz Zone.*"

Jake smiled modestly. "Yeah."

"You were on that show twice, am I right?"

"Correct."

"You did better the first time."

"He knows," said Kojo while Jake said, "I know."

"So will you take us downriver?" asked Grace.

"You're kids." The man rubbed his thumb against his fingers. "Who's going to pay me?"

"Me," said Grace.

She pulled out an American Express Black Card.

Whoa, thought Jake. He knew you needed to have an annual income of at least one million dollars to score one of those.

The charter captain's eyes bulged when he saw the black Amex card.

"Are we good?" asked Grace.

"Totally," said Captain Grumby. "Hop aboard, kids. Strap on your life vests. Let's go chase us a pirate ship!"

65

The single-sail sloop was swift.

But the *Stinky Dog II* was still a good half mile downstream of Jake and his friends.

"Can we please go a little faster, Captain Grumby?" shouted Grace.

"Why? What's the rush? Enjoy the scenery. Smell that breeze. She's blowing hard today."

"And we're going to blow our chance to catch that yacht if we don't step on the gas!" hollered Kojo.

"No gas, man," said Captain Grumby. "Just wind. This is a *sail*boat. We use the natural elements of nature. I maintain a very light carbon footprint—"

"Captain?" said Jake. "Might I suggest we initiate tacking? A zigzag pattern against this blustery breeze. By picking the right vectors, we can make this sailboat fly faster than the wind!"

"Go for it, kid!" said the captain. "I, uh, missed that vector class at sailboat school."

Jake took the wheel.

"Crank the winch, Kojo. Pull the line tight and secure it. We'll swing the boom starboard."

Kojo secured the sail. Jake turned the wheel, hand over hand. Grace tried not to get seasick.

There were more zigs. More zags. They tacked to port. They tacked to starboard. The power of the wind pulled them faster and faster.

"We're gaining on them!" shouted Captain Grumby.

The sloop was really clipping along, listing a little to the side every time Jake zigged or zagged. Kojo kept working the winches. The boom kept swinging. Grace kept trying not to hurl.

As they headed out into the bay and cut across the *Stinky Dog*'s wake near the Statue of Liberty, the gap between the vessels suddenly collapsed.

"They've shut down their engines," said Grace, who was hanging off a railing. "They're dropping anchor."

Frankie, the Consortium guy who, once upon a time, had driven Jake to Zinkle Inkle, strode to the stern of the yacht and lowered an aluminum ladder.

"Hello, Jake," he said. "Good to see you again."

"Nice of you to join us," said Dr. Doublé as she stepped up to the railing beside Frankie.

"You stole our diamonds!" shouted Grace.

"Whoa!" said Captain Grumby. "Is that how you

scored that Amex Black Card? You're a diamond dealer? Because I'm thinking about getting my lady friend a little somethin'. . . ."

Grace was too furious with Dr. Doublé to respond.

"They're our diamonds now," said Dr. Doublé.

"No, they are not!"

Dr. Doublé smirked. "Are you familiar with the legal theory of 'finderus keeperus, loserus weeperus'?"

"And," said Kojo, "are you familiar with the term 'you're busted, baby'? Because we're gonna call our friends at the FBI. Right now. Isn't that right, Captain Grumby."

The charter-boat captain patted his pockets.

"Oops," he said. "We left the dock so quickly, I forgot to grab my VHF ship-to-shore radio."

"Well, I have my phone," said Kojo. He glanced at the screen. "And there are absolutely no bars out here, because the Statue of Liberty isn't a cell-phone tower."

"She's also about to lose her torch," said Dr. Doublé.

"Excuse me?" said Grace.

"Hubert couldn't make our laser weapon fully operational. However, he was able to tweak it to the point that its beam could easily slice through Lady Liberty's right wrist."

"You wouldn't dare!" said Grace.

"Wouldn't I?" snickered Dr. Doublé. "I need some sort of demonstration to prove to the world the power of the weapon I am offering for sale. Slicing off the Statue of

Liberty's torch hand would be a far more effective demo than demolishing a water tank on top of a school."

"That was Hubert Huxley's idea, right?" said Jake.

"Yes. Poor boy. He really does hate that school."

"Well, then he should run for the student council," said Kojo. "Try to become the change he wants to see."

Dr. Doublé ignored him. Her eyes were laser focused on Jake.

"Of course, Mr. McQuade, you might give us a reason to change our plans regarding Lady Liberty."

"What do you mean?" asked Jake.

"Simple. We both knew this day would come. No one else can make our space laser all it might be. The Consortium requires your assistance, Jake. We need your big, beautiful brain!"

66

"Your choice, Mr. McQuade," gloated Dr. Doublé. "You help us, or Lady Liberty loses a limb. Maybe a pointy piece of her crown."

Jake's brain was whirling faster than a washing machine in the spin cycle.

Buy time, he told himself. *Play along. If the game is still going, you still have a chance to win.*

"Okay," said Jake. "I'm coming aboard your vessel. I'll see what I can do to help you optimize your . . . project. But Grace and Kojo go back to the dock with Captain Grumby."

"No," said Dr. Doublé. "They do not. How foolish do you think I am? Your friends would simply contact your other friends. The ones at the FBI and the CIA."

"Actually," said Kojo, "I was just going to call Everett

260

Robertson. He's a big cheese down at the Office of the Director of National Intelligence because, hello, he *is* the director of national intelligence."

"Silence!" hissed Dr. Doublé. "Captain?"

Captain Grumby looked around for someone else to be the captain of his sloop. "Oh, you mean me?"

"Grab a line. You will tie your ship off to ours. We will tow it out to sea. You're coming with us, too."

The sailboat was tethered to the yacht. Jake, Kojo, Grace, and Captain Grumby all reluctantly climbed up the ladder.

"My lady friend is going to be so mad," grumbled Captain Grumby. "We have reservations at the Mermaid Inn. Their lobster rolls are awesome, man."

The four hostages were hustled across the deck and into the party room.

"Sweet," said Captain Grumby, looking up and admiring the mirror ball hanging from the ceiling. "I might catch disco fever in here."

Four of Dr. Doublé's minions—Amir, Eddie, Frankie, and Nikos—snarled at him.

Captain Grumby didn't say much after that.

Dr. Doublé tapped an intercom button.

"Full speed ahead, Betina," she said. "Take us out to sea. Mr. McQuade is going to cooperate with us. Because he doesn't want to see any of his friends get hurt. Isn't that right, Jake?"

"You know," said Jake, "if I'm not home in time for supper, my mom will be very worried. She might start calling people."

"Mine, too," said Grace and Kojo.

"Betina?" Dr. Doublé shouted into the intercom up to the bridge. "Drop anchor as soon as we pass under the bridge. It appears we have a deadline. Mr. McQuade has to optimize our laser blaster before his dinner goes cold."

"Actually," said Jake, "I'm usually the one cooking dinner. So it'd be great if I was home by, let's say, five. Five-thirty at the latest."

"What's on the menu tonight?" asked Grace.

"Not sure. Maybe my cheesy spaghetti pie . . ."

"Oh, that's a good one, baby," said Kojo.

"Enough!" shrieked Dr. Doublé.

She swung out her arm and pointed at what looked like a four-foot orb constructed with K'NEX rods sitting in the center of the dance floor.

The skeletal sphere most resembled one of those expandable and collapsible geodesic domes known as Hoberman spheres. Jake figured it was made out of a lightweight but sturdy composite. Something that would work in space.

Dozens of lasers were clamped to the struts. And there, suspended in the center, were the two diamonds, the orange and the red. The gemstones' job was to bring the multiple beams together to produce one intensely powerful, focused laser blast. The firing lens was pointed toward an open window and the ocean beyond.

"So what seems to be the problem?" asked Jake, sounding like an automobile mechanic.

"Hubert was unable to align the diamond facets properly."

"Is that so?" said Jake as he rolled up his sleeves and studied the two giant diamonds at the center of what Jake knew was a polyhedron with twenty triangular faces and twelve pentagonal faces.

Yup! Not a single one of his jelly beans had worn off.

"Okay," he said. "Let's optimize this bad boy. Let's optimize it good."

67

Jake was doing all sorts of high-level geometry in his head, figuring out the angles for his upcoming billiard shot.

He thought about all the gem- and candy-blasting games he used to play on his phone. He was going to need those skills as well as his understanding of the law of reflection (the angle at which an object strikes its reflective medium is equal to the angle at which it bounces off).

"Okay," he said, "I need you folks to stand in a circle around the device. Once you're in position, do not move."

"Why not?" asked Dr. Doublé.

Jake could tell she didn't totally trust him.

"Because," said Jake with an exaggerated sigh, as if he was soooo tired of explaining things, "I am going to be making incremental adjustments to the orientation of both diamonds, and any light shift instigated by body movement could recalibrate dispersion due to refraction!"

Everybody in the room was slack-jawed when Jake finished.

He'd punked them all. He'd spewed a bunch of gibberish—with just a hint of actual scientific fact.

The crowd of bad guys quickly shuffled into place around the laser-studded frame.

"Grace? Kojo? I need you two on the power switch. Kindly take it behind the counter over there and wait for my signal. Captain Grumby? You move behind the bar, too."

"Cool," said Captain Grumby.

"Why do they need to move the power switch?" asked Dr. Doublé.

Jake gave her an exaggerated eye roll. "Have you never read anything by your renowned countryman René Descartes? He independently derived his reflection law using heuristic momentum-conservation arguments while simultaneously inventing analytic geometry!"

Dr. Doublé couldn't keep up with Jake's rapid-fire brain dump. He was having fun, jumbling up stuff that, thanks to Mr. Farooqi's IK capsules, he had imprinted on his brain.

He made his eyes bug open wide. He tugged at his hair to make it look more mad-scientist-ish. "Once I begin my micro-adjustments, you must all remain absolutely still, or the whole thing will be ruined! Ruined, I tell you!"

"Okay, kid, okay," said Frankie, who'd taken up a position in the ring around the laser ball. "But lay off the lectures. If I wanted to know stuff, I woulda stayed in school."

The henchpeople facing the bar were giving Jake's friends and the sailboat captain some seriously evil looks. He wished he could tell his friends what he was up to.

But he couldn't. They'd just have to trust that he knew what he was doing.

And Jake just had to trust that he could do it!

68

Now it was time for some intense internal trigonometry.

Jake noted where the five bad guys were standing. He flexed his fingers to limber them up. He was so glad he had two diamonds to fidget with.

For this to work, he'd need both faceted rocks.

"You guys ready?" he called to Kojo, Grace, and Captain Grumby.

"Be careful, Jake!" shouted Grace. "You don't have to do this, you know."

"Yeah, I kind of do."

He leaned in and, with visions of vectors and angles dancing in his head, adjusted the giant orange diamond to its optimal position. Fortunately, the thing was huge. It had a lot of flat, reflective planes. He'd need five of them.

One for every player from the other team currently in the party room.

Next he worked with the Red Lion Diamond. This was, hopefully, going to be just like the time he and Kojo used the binocular prism to defeat the lasers on that field test with the Consortium.

And the mirror ball directly overhead?

It was part of the plan, too.

Everything was ready.

This was his one big chance.

"Power up!" he shouted to Kojo.

"Roger that!" Kojo shouted back.

"Powering up!" added Grace.

"Ducking down!" shouted Captain Grumby.

Jake heard a heavy thump.

The array of lasers hummed and whirred to life.

Pinpoints of light emerged around the rim of the expanded orb in a constellation of piercing red stars.

Jake dropped to the floor just as multiple beams hit the Red Lion Diamond. But instead of doing what Dr. Doublé dreamed of, instead of being focused into one single, powerful beam shot through the weapon's lens, the lasers bounced back to their sources, frying their circuitry, knocking them out.

In the same instant, the multiple beams bouncing off la Gran Calabaza shot upward to hit the five mirror squares on the disco ball that Jake had targeted. Those beams ricocheted down and zapped every single one of the bad guys and Dr. Doublé.

Stung by the laser blasts, the henchpeople jerked backward reflexively and tumbled to the floor.

Dr. Doublé's hands flew up to her stylish silk scarf, which had a hole singed through it. Her hair was scorched, too.

"Youch!" screamed Frankie, whose wristwatch was sizzling. "That stings!"

"You've destroyed our Death Star!" shrieked Dr. Doublé.

"You burned a hole in the seat of my pants!" shouted Amir.

"Seize him!" cried Frankie as he attempted to stand on his wobbly legs. "Seize them all!"

But before any of them could make a move, they were distracted by the crackling, popping, and snapping sound of the expandable dome collapsing on itself. Everybody shielded their faces as reflected beams that weren't destroying their sources of origin sliced and burned through the frame, sending up a shower of sparks and smoke.

"You will pay for this, Jake McQuade!" shouted Dr. Doublé. "You will pay!"

"No problem," said Jake.

"Yeah," said Kojo. "Grace has an awesome credit card."

Grace nodded. "There's no preset spending limit."

That's when Jake heard the heavy *whomp-whomp-whomp* of helicopter rotors overhead.

Party-deck windows started shattering.

Someone else was boarding the boat!

69

Heavy boots slammed through the rectangular windows lining both sides of the yacht.

A dozen SWAT-team commandos using rappelling gear and ropes swung onto the dance floor and surrounded Dr. Doublé's minions.

"Freeze!" shouted one. "FBI!"

The bad guys thrust their arms up into the air.

Two members of the FBI team tilted back the visors on their tactical helmets.

Special Agents Andrus and Otis.

"Secure the bridge," Andrus said into his shoulder-mounted walkie-talkie.

"The bridge is secure," came the tinny reply.

"Well done, guys," Otis said to Jake, Grace, and Kojo. "You too, sir," she added.

"Thanks, man," said Captain Grumby. "Happy to

be of service. These gnarly dudes wanted to slice off the Statue of Liberty's torch hand."

"How'd you find us?" asked Jake.

"Deputy Assistant Director Struchen's tech people noticed how many times you called your personal hotline," said Andrus. "So we checked in with Special Agent Karen Duggan."

"The new school secretary?"

Otis winked. "She's one of ours."

"Hey, we told you we were going to beef up your security detail after that incident on Liberty Island," added Agent Andrus.

"Mrs. Duggan is an undercover operative?" said Kojo. "That is so cool!"

"She left her post in the school office, tracked your movements," said Andrus. "She saw you board the sailboat."

"That's mine," said Captain Grumby, raising his hand.

"Fortunately," said Otis, "we already had the helicopter with the rappelling gear standing by."

Andrus nodded. "Standard urban deployment package."

"So," said Otis, surveying the pack of semi-scorched villains. "Who have we here?"

"She's the kingpin," said Kojo. "The evil genius known as Dr. Doublé. She claims to be French. I wouldn't trust her on that. I wouldn't trust her on anything. The rest of these saps are just her nefarious henchpeople."

"Where's Hubert Huxley?" asked Andrus.

"That slacker?" sneered Dr. Doublé. "He's down below. Taking a nap."

"Guess stealing the Red Lion Diamond from the school wore him out," added Kojo.

Both FBI agents looked surprised.

"That's right," said Kojo. "We closed that case for you, too. You're welcome."

"And, as you already know," said Grace, "Dr. Doublé worked with Zane Zinkle to steal my family's other diamond, la Gran Calabaza."

"And where is Mr. Zinkle?" asked Otis.

"We don't know," said Jake. "Sorry."

"If I cooperate and help you find him," said Dr. Doublé, "will you cut me a deal?"

"Maybe," said Andrus.

"Maybe not," said Otis.

"Seriously?" Kojo scoffed at Dr. Doublé. "Come on, lady. You were trying to build your own Death Star!"

"Ooh!" said Agent Otis. "Like from *Star Wars*?"

"Yep," said Jake. "But unfortunately they lost their focus. So did their laser beams. They bounced all over the place!"

Grace and Kojo laughed.

"Good one, man," said Kojo.

"Welcome back," Grace added with a wink.

Jake smiled.

Because he felt like his old self. Only super intelligent, too.

Hey, who ever said being a genius couldn't be fun?

70

FBI agents escorted Dr. Doublé and the others off the yacht in handcuffs.

Hubert woke up in the bedroom cabin looking rumpled and disheveled.

"He's the one who stole the Red Lion Diamond?" asked Agent Otis.

"Indeed, I am," said Hubert, proudly.

"Uh, I think you just confessed, big guy," said Kojo.

"I disagree," said Hubert. "I am merely taking credit for masterminding a brilliant heist."

"How'd you crack the security code?" asked Agent Andrus.

"I have absolutely no recollection of doing that," sniffed Hubert. "I just remember stealing the diamond."

"You did it again," said Kojo.

"You really only need to confess once," said Grace.

"So, Hubert?" said Jake, because he really needed to know one thing.

"What?"

"Where you're going, they may not have candy. Would you like us to grab you something? Maybe a bag of jelly beans?"

"Jelly beans? Heavens, no. I loathe and despise those cloying rainbow pellets of Easter Bunny poop."

Jake breathed a sigh of relief. His secret was safe. So was Mr. Farooqi's. Hubert Huxley had forgotten all about the jelly beans he'd stolen and how he'd temporarily become the smartest kid in the universe.

Hubert laughed. Grace, Kojo, and Jake took a giant step backward to avoid the stench.

"Jelly beans. Why on earth would I want jelly beans?"

Jake shrugged. "I dunno. I kind of like 'em."

"Because, smart as you might be, McQuade, you're also extremely foolish and seriously immature."

"Yeah," said Jake, smiling broadly. "I guess I am. And you know what?"

"What?"

"I like it that way."

"Me too," said Grace.

"Yin and yang, baby," said Kojo. "Yin and yang."

* * *

Hubert was taken to a juvenile detention facility and immediately sent to the dentist to have his teeth cleaned. The dentist also prescribed an extremely powerful mouthwash.

Dr. Doublé and her minions were held without bail pending trial. They would probably spend the rest of their lives in prison.

Mrs. Penelope Flippington Huxley was temporarily held and released, because she really hadn't committed any crimes. Her chauffeur, Chauncy, wasn't so lucky. He was put in the same jail as the rest of Dr. Doublé's crew.

Zane Zinkle remained at large. There were a few unconfirmed sightings posted on social media. The most recent had him working at a car wash outside Schenectady.

Clear of any legal charges, Mrs. Huxley launched a custody battle over la Gran Calabaza with Grace Garcia and her uncle Charley Lyons. But the judge agreed with Grace's argument before the court.

The giant orange diamond was donated to the American Museum of Natural History's Hall of Gems and Minerals so millions of people could see what had been lost to the world for over three centuries.

A week after the events in New York Harbor, Haazim Farooqi invited Jake, Grace, and Kojo up to his lab for an update on his newest batch of jelly beans.

"The tutti-frutti bean was not from the jar you

devoured backstage at the Imperial Marquis Hotel, Subject One!" he announced.

"How can you tell?" asked Jake.

"I found my old briefcase," he said, holding up another double-handled plastic shopping bag. "The one I carried to the hotel that fateful night when you gobbled down my prototype IK capsules."

"Are you sure?" asked Grace.

"Yes. Inside this bag is nothing but the book I had wanted to have autographed by the eminent futurist Dr. Blackbridge. But he would not give me the time of day."

Jake grinned. "His loss, Mr. Farooqi."

"Big time," added Kojo.

"So the tutti-frutti jelly bean was from either the second or third batch," said Farooqi.

"Judging by what happened to Hubert Huxley," said Jake, "how he fell back to his prior level of intelligence, I'm pretty sure it was the third."

"Agreed. Suffice it to say, your jelly beans, from my original recipe, will not perform—or, more accurately, not fail to perform—in the same manner as those gobbled down by Hubert Huxley. You, Subject One, remain good to go. For now. Nothing is ever one hundred percent, except, perhaps, your scores on a math test."

"We should celebrate!" said Jake.

"Let's do it!" added Kojo.

"Woo-hoo!" shouted Grace.

Mr. Farooqi ordered chicken karahi and biryani for everybody. He also broke out the Chillz Chatpata potato sticks and lots of Shezan fruit drinks.

"We have done much, Subject One," Farooqi said with a burp. "And we have much more to do!"

"Then," said Jake with a burp of his own, "let's do it!"

In the car ride home, Jake sat between Grace and Kojo in the back seat.

"I'm glad we didn't make this driver wait," said Kojo. "They charge for that, you know."

"Yeah," said Jake. "I know."

"Hey, Jake?" said Grace, grabbing his hand.

"Uh, yeah?" said Jake nervously, because, hello, Grace Garcia was holding his hand.

"Remember that thing you said about energy being the only thing that doesn't change?"

"Sure. The total amount of energy and matter in the universe remains constant. It merely changes from one form to another. Do you guys know the first law of thermodynamics?"

"No," said Kojo. "What's the first law of thermodynamics?"

"Don't play with matches."

Grace laughed.

"Of course, the second law states—"

Grace placed a finger to her lips.

Jake took the hint and quit yammering.

"You know what else I hope never changes?" asked Grace.

Jake shook his head.

Grace smiled.

"You, Jake McQuade. You!"

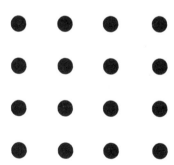

BONUS PUZZLE!
Are you as good at bouncing laser beams
and hitting targets as Jake McQuade,
the smartest kid in the universe?

Let's find out.

Can you connect all sixteen dots with no more than six
laser-straight lines **without lifting your pen or pencil or
retracing your path?**

Good luck! (You might want to eat a few jelly beans
before you start.)

Go to chrisgrabenstein.com to check your answer!

Thank You . . .

To my extremely talented wife (and coauthor of *Shine!*), J.J. She reads everything before anyone else and always encourages me to cut the boring stuff. Marrying her was the smartest thing I've ever done.

To Shana Corey, my longtime editor at Random House. If J.J. misses any slow parts, Shana catches them. Shana and I have done over a dozen books together, and she is the brilliant offstage voice making me look better in the spotlight.

To Tia Resham Cheema, Shana's bright new editorial assistant. I can already tell Tia's been eating her jelly beans.

To my extremely nimble-witted literary agents, Carrie Hannigan and Josh Getzler, plus everybody at HG Literary. They take care of the business stuff so I can focus on the silly stuff.

To our very clever cover artist, Antoine Losty. He's done all three Smartest Kid books and continues to outdo himself every time.

To Neil Swaab, who designed our very smart-looking title lettering.

To the authenticity readers who helped me with this book: Barbara Perez Marquez and Brittany N. Williams.

To the whole brainy Random House Children's Books team: John Adamo, Barbara Bakowski, Natalie Capogrossi, Katrina Damkoehler, Kathleen Dunn, Emily DuVal, Lili Feinberg, Janet Foley, Katie Halata, Kate Keating, Alison Kolani, Mallory Loehr, Barbara Marcus, Kelly McGauley, Michelle Nagler, Catherine O'Mara, Jinna Shin, Erica Stone, Tim Terhune, Jen Valero, Megan Shortt, Rebecca Vitkus, Adrienne Waintraub, and April Ward.

To the percipient publicists at Blue Slip Media, Barbara Fisch and Sarah Shealy.

To the entire savvy sales team at Random House Children's Books. Thank you for working so hard to get the right books into the right kids' hands.

To all the brilliant booksellers, big and small, who have supported my work over the years.

And finally, thank you, Mom, for encouraging me to move from Tennessee to New York City way back in 1979, when I was just a kid with big dreams, a big imagination, and the typewriter you gave me for my high school graduation.

CHRIS GRABENSTEIN

is the #1 *New York Times* bestselling author of the hilarious and award-winning Mr. Lemoncello's Library, Dog Squad, Smartest Kid in the Universe, and Welcome to Wonderland series. He's also written *The Island of Dr. Libris, Shine!* (coauthored with J.J. Grabenstein), and many, many other books and plays. Chris enjoys jelly beans but has never once contemplated world domination (except when playing Risk with his four brothers). Chris lives in New York City with his wife, J.J., and their cats, Luigi and Phoebe Squeak. Visit chrisgrabenstein.com for trailers, puzzle solutions, teaching materials, and more!

@cgrabenstein
cgrabber1955
chris.grabenstein

DISCOVER THE WACKY WORLD OF LEMONCELLO. . . .

A *New York Times* bestselling series

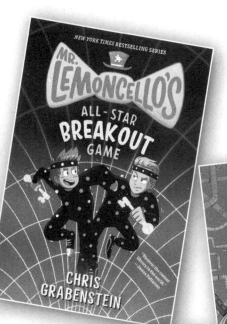

IS IT FUN? HELLO! IT'S A LEMONCELLO!

Turn the page for a sneak peek at Book 1.

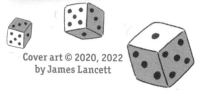

Cover art © 2020, 2022
by James Lancett

This is how Kyle Keeley got grounded for a week.

First he took a shortcut through his mother's favorite rosebush.

Yes, the thorns hurt, but having crashed through the brambles and trampled a few petunias, he had a five-second jump on his oldest brother, Mike.

Both Kyle and his big brother knew exactly where to find what they needed to win the game: inside the house!

Kyle had already found the pinecone to complete his "outdoors" round. And he was pretty sure Mike had snagged his "yellow flower." Hey, it was June. Dandelions were everywhere.

"Give it up, Kyle!" shouted Mike as the brothers dashed up the driveway. "You don't stand a chance."

Mike zoomed past Kyle and headed for the front door, wiping out Kyle's temporary lead.

Of course he did.

Seventeen-year-old Mike Keeley was a total jock, a high school superstar. Football, basketball, baseball. If it had a ball, Mike Keeley was good at it.

Kyle, who was twelve, wasn't the star of anything.

Kyle's other brother, Curtis, who was fifteen, was still trapped over in the neighbor's yard, dealing with their dog. Curtis was the smartest Keeley. But for *his* "outdoors" round, he had pulled the always unfortunate Your Neighbor's Dog's Toy card. Any "dog" card was basically the same as a Lose a Turn.

As for why the three Keeley brothers were running around their neighborhood on a Sunday afternoon like crazed lunatics, grabbing all sorts of wacky stuff, well, it was their mother's fault.

She was the one who had suggested, "If you boys are bored, play a board game!"

So Kyle had gone down into the basement and dug up one of his all-time favorites: Mr. Lemoncello's Indoor-Outdoor Scavenger Hunt. It had been a huge hit for Mr. Lemoncello, the master game maker. Kyle and his brothers had played it so much when they were younger, Mrs. Keeley wrote to Mr. Lemoncello's company for a refresher pack of clue cards. The new cards listed all sorts of different bizarro stuff you needed to find, like "an adult's droopy underpants," "one dirty dish," and "a rotten banana peel."

(At the end of the game, the losers had to put everything back exactly where the items had been found. It was an official rule, printed inside the top of the box, and made winning the game that much more important!)

While Curtis was stranded next door, trying to talk the neighbor's Doberman, Twinky, out of his favorite tug toy, Kyle and Mike were both searching for the same two items, because for the final round, all the players were given the same Riddle Card.

That day's riddle, even though it was a card Kyle had never seen before, had been extra easy.

FIND TWO COINS FROM 1982 THAT ADD UP TO THIRTY CENTS AND ONE OF THEM CANNOT BE A NICKEL.

Duh. The answer was a quarter and a nickel because the riddle said only *one* of them couldn't be a nickel.

So to win, Kyle had to find a 1982 quarter *and* a 1982 nickel.

Also easy.

Their dad kept an apple cider jug filled with loose change down in his basement workshop.

That's why Kyle and Mike were racing to get there first.

Mike bolted through the front door.

Kyle grinned.

He loved playing games against his big brothers. As the youngest, it was just about the only chance he ever got to beat them fair and square. Board games leveled the playing field. You needed a good roll of the dice, a lucky draw of the cards, and some smarts, but if things went your way and you gave it your all, anyone could win.

Especially today, since Mike had blown his lead by choosing the standard route down to the basement. He'd go through the front door, tear to the back of the house, bound down the steps, and then run to their dad's workshop.

Kyle, on the other hand, would take a shortcut.

He hopped over a couple of boxy shrubs and kicked open the low-to-the-ground casement window. He heard something crackle when his tennis shoe hit the windowpane, but he couldn't worry about it. He had to beat his big brother.

He crawled through the narrow opening, dropped to the floor, and scrabbled over to the workbench, where he found the jug, dumped out the coins, and started sifting through the sea of pennies, nickels, dimes, and quarters.

Score!

Kyle quickly uncovered a 1982 nickel. He tucked it into his shirt pocket and sent pennies, nickels, and dimes skidding across the floor as he concentrated on quarters. 2010. 2003. 1986.

"Come on, come on," he muttered.

The workshop door swung open.

"What the . . . ?" Mike was surprised to see that Kyle had beaten him to the coin jar.

Mike fell to his knees and started searching for his own

coins just as Kyle shouted, "Got it!" and plucked a 1982 quarter out of the pile.

"What about the nickel?" demanded Mike.

Kyle pulled it out of his shirt pocket.

"You went through the window?" said a voice from outside.

It was Curtis. Kneeling in the flower beds.

"Yeah," said Kyle.

"I was going to do that. The shortest distance between two points is a straight line."

"I can't believe you won!" moaned Mike, who wasn't used to losing *anything*.

"Well," said Kyle, standing up and strutting a little, "believe it, brother. Because now you two *losers* have to put all the junk back."

"I am *not* taking this back to Twinky!" said Curtis. He held up a very slimy, knotted rope.

"Oh, yes you are," said Kyle. "Because you *lost*. Oh sure, you *thought* about using the window. . . ."

"Um, Kyle?" mumbled Curtis. "You might want to shut up. . . ."

"What? C'mon, Curtis. Don't be such a sore loser. Just because I was the one who took the shortcut and kicked open the window and—"

"You did this, Kyle?"

A new face appeared in the window.

Their dad's.

"Heh, heh, heh," chuckled Mike behind Kyle.

"You broke the glass?" Their father sounded ticked off. "Well, guess who's going to pay to have this window replaced."

That's why Kyle Keeley had fifty cents deducted from his allowance for the rest of the year.

And got grounded for a week.

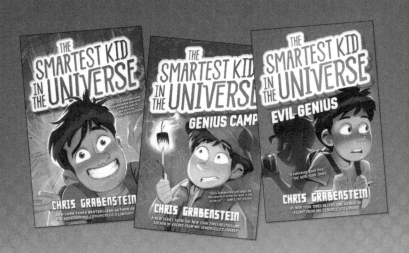